The Best Western Stories of
BILL PRONZINI

The Western Writers series is edited
by Bill Pronzini and Martin H. Greenberg

ALSO IN THE SERIES

The Best Western Stories of Steve Frazee

The Best Western Stories of Wayne D. Overholser

The Best Western Stories of Frank Bonham

The Best Western Stories of Loren D. Estleman

The Best Western Stories of Lewis B. Patten

The Best Western Stories of
BILL PRONZINI

EDITED BY BILL PRONZINI

AND MARTIN H. GREENBERG

SWALLOW PRESS

OHIO UNIVERSITY PRESS

ATHENS

Introduction copyright © 1990 by
Robert E. Briney

Swallow Press/Ohio University Press
books are printed on acid-free paper. ∞

Printed in the United States of America.
All rights reserved.

Library of Congress Cataloging-in-Publication Data

Pronzini, Bill.
   The best western stories of Bill Pronzini / edited by Bill Pronzini and Martin H. Greenberg.
      p. cm.
   ISBN 0-8040-0932-5
   1. Western stories. I. Greenberg, Martin Henry. II. Title.
PS3566.R67A6   1990   813'.54—dc20   89-21778

Designed by Laury A. Egan

Contents

Acknowledgments	vii
Introduction: No Easy Answers: Bill Pronzini BY ROBERT E. BRINEY	ix
The Gambler	1
Markers	12
Wooden Indian	20
Righteous Guns	36
Fergus O'Hara, Detective	41
All the Long Years	71
Decision	82
Cave of Ice (with Marcia Muller)	91
The Hanging Man	101
Hero	117
McIntosh's Chute	125
Fyfe and the Drummers	139
No Room at the Inn	147
The Western Pulps	162
A Bibliography of Books by Bill Pronzini	171

Acknowledgments

"The Gambler." Copyright © 1989 by Bill Pronzini. First published in *New Frontiers I*.

"Markers." Copyright © 1982 by Western Writers of America, Inc. First published in the anthology *Roundup*.

"Wooden Indian." Copyright © 1989 by Davis Publications, Inc. First published in *Alfred Hitchcock's Mystery Magazine*.

"Righteous Guns." Copyright © 1990 by Bill Pronzini.

"Fergus O'Hara, Detective." Copyright © 1974 by H.S.D. Publications, Inc.; © 1976 by Jack Foxx. First published in *Alfred Hitchcock's Mystery Magazine*. Revised version copyright © 1990 by Bill Pronzini.

"All the Long Years." Copyright © 1988 by Bill Pronzini. First published in *Westeryear*.

"Decision." Copyright © 1971 by Zane Grey Western Magazine, Inc.; copyright © 1983 by Bill Pronzini. First published in *Zane Grey Western Magazine*.

"Cave of Ice." Copyright © 1986 by the Boy Scouts of America. First published in *Boys' Life*.

"The Hanging Man." Copyright © 1981 by Bill Pronzini. First published in *Ellery Queen's Mystery Magazine*.

"Hero." Copyright © 1988 by Bill Pronzini. First published in *Small Felonies*.

ACKNOWLEDGMENTS

"McIntosh's Chute." Copyright © 1989 by Bill Pronzini. First published in *New Frontiers I* as by Jack Foxx.

"Fyfe and the Drummers." Copyright © 1990 by Bill Pronzini.

"No Room at the Inn." Copyright © 1988 by Bill Pronzini. First published in *Crime at Christmas*.

"The Western Pulps." Copyright © 1986, 1990 by Bill Pronzini. Portions of this article first appeared as part of the Introduction to *Wild Westerns*, edited by Bill Pronzini.

"Introduction: No Easy Answers: Bill Pronzini." Copyright © 1990 by Robert E. Briney.

Introduction

No Easy Answers: Bill Pronzini

BY ROBERT E. BRINEY

"I don't like guns much."
—*Bill Pronzini*

OVER A SPAN of twenty-three years he has published more than forty novels and two hundred and fifty short stories, plus a large body of critical commentary and reviews, and has edited or co-edited so many anthologies that it is difficult to keep track of them all. He has collaborated extensively and successfully with a variety of other writers, and his work has appeared under eleven pen names in addition to his own name. He is widely regarded as one of the best contemporary American mystery writers, mainly for his series of seventeen (so far) novels about a nameless San Francisco-based private detective. He has had stories included in twelve out of the past eighteen volumes of the *Best Detective Stories of the Year* and its successor series, *The Year's Best Mystery and Suspense Stories*. He was the guest of honor at the fifteenth annual Anthony Boucher Memorial Mystery Convention ("Boucher-

INTRODUCTION

con") in 1984. His novel *Hoodwink* (1981) and short story "Cat's-Paw" (1983), both featuring the "Nameless Detective," won best-of-the-year awards from the Private Eye Writers of America, and the same organization presented him with its Life Achievement Award in 1987. And, as several critics have observed, he continues to grow from story to story and book to book, setting new challenges for himself and providing new satisfactions for his readers.

William John Pronzini was born in Petaluma, California, on 13 April 1943. He knew from an early age that he wanted to be a writer: at the age of twelve he wrote a juvenile ("very juvenile") mystery called *The Devil's Island Mystery*. But it was not until the mid-1960s, after two years at a junior college and an assortment of short-lived jobs, that he began a systematic assault on the fiction market. His first published story was "You Don't Know What It's Like" in the final issue (November 1966) of *Shell Scott's Mystery Magazine*. His stories were soon appearing in *Mike Shayne Mystery Magazine* and most of the other digest-sized crime-fiction magazines. Over the years, more than fifty stories appeared in *Alfred Hitchcock's Mystery Magazine* and twenty-five in *Ellery Queen's Mystery Magazine*. The bulk of this work was in the mystery/detective field, a natural consequence of the fact that Pronzini had long been a reader and collector of mystery pulp magazines and books. But he also wrote Westerns for *Zane Grey Western Magazine* and science fiction, fantasy, and horror fiction for *Analog*, *The Magazine of Fantasy and Science Fiction*, *Fantastic*, and *Coven 13*.

Pronzini became a full-time writer in 1969. He has always been known for his success in collaborating with other writers, and his most frequent collaborator in the 1970s was Jeffrey M. Wallmann. In addition to their own names and the joint byline "William Jeffrey," they wrote under several "house names." As "Robert Hart Davis" they wrote about Charlie Chan for the short-lived *Charlie Chan Mystery Magazine*, and as "Brett Halliday" they produced one Mike Shayne novella for the magazine named after that character. With science fiction writer Barry N. Malzberg, Pronzini wrote science fiction and horror stories and such books as *The Running of Beasts* (1976), an exceptionally effective novel of terror.

Pronzini's first novel, *The Stalker*, was published in 1971. That same year saw the appearance of the first "Nameless Detective" novel, *The Snatch*, based on a short story of the same title. After some irregularity in the 1970s, the series has now settled down to approximately one novel per year. "Nameless" is an immensely appealing character: tough when the occasion demands, but with a full measure of sympathy and compassion for the victims of crime. He is not a disinterested observer or an impersonal instrument of justice. He has a fully developed personal life, which is of as much interest as the details of the crimes he investigates. As the reviewer for *Ellery Queen's Mystery Magazine* wrote, "The reader's involvement with 'Nameless' and his problems continues to increase in intensity, making [the series] succeed on an emotional level rare in the field."

Like his creator, "Nameless" does not like guns much. That terse statement (or understatement) in fact represents a philosophy that informs much of Pronzini's work, the Westerns as well as the crime fiction. As the Chicago *Sun-Times* put it: "His novels are cerebral, not bloody. There is violence, but of a muted sort, and none of it is gratuitous. The 'Nameless' novels are a thinking reader's detective series." And *Library Journal* said, "Pronzini writes about violence with horror; his murder mysteries make readers aware of the ravages visited upon people by casual killing."

At their (frequent) best, Pronzini's stories do not opt for the easy solutions. Not for him the convenient confession and suicide that clears up the mystery, or the climactic gun-battle

INTRODUCTION

that neatly disposes of the villains. Many of the characters in Pronzini's fiction must live with and deal with their own flaws and with the consequences of their past actions. Like the protagonist of at least one of the stories in the present collection, they can find themselves boxed into a tragic situation with no solution in sight.

This brings us, in somewhat roundabout fashion, to a closer examination of Pronzini's Western fiction.

His first published Western fiction was a short story, "Sawtooth Justice," in the November 1969 issue of *Zane Grey Western Magazine* (the second incarnation of that title). Over the next four years, until the magazine ceased publication in 1973, some twenty stories by Pronzini appeared in its pages. Half a dozen of these, collaborations with Jeffrey Wallmann under the "Romer Zane Grey" house name, were based on characters created by Zane Grey: the Indian Yaqui in one story and Arizona Ames in the other five. ("Dreadful stuff," Pronzini says now.) Most of the other stories deal with traditional Western themes, though not always in expected ways. For example, "The Posse from Paytonville" in the June 1970 issue explores the reactions of the teenaged protagonist when the posse with which he is riding turns into a lynch mob. Another story, "'I'll See to Your Horse'," would later become the basis for the novel *The Gallows Land*. "Decision," in the present collection, is a revised version of this story.

The magazine market for Western short stories had disappeared by the late 1970s, so Pronzini eventually turned his attention to book-length works. Two Western novels written in collaboration with Jeffrey Wallmann appeared in the early 1980s. Published under the byline "William Jeffrey," they were issued as paperbacks in the U.S. and in hardcover in England. *Duel at Gold Buttes* (1981), set in the Dakota badlands, is the story of Jim Glencannon, framed for the murder of a friend and on the run from the local sheriff, who unmasks the real killers with the help of the dead man's widow and young son. In *Border Fever* (1983), Territorial Ranger Oak M'Candliss must deal with revolutionaries and with a gang of murderous bandits on the Arizona-Mexico border. Both novels are fast-paced examples of, as Pronzini now says, "pure pulp."

Pronzini's first solo Western novel was the previously mentioned *The Gallows Land* (Walker, 1983). Roy Boone, formerly a farmer but now rootless and wandering after the death of his wife, stops to ask for water at a run-down ranch in the Arizona desert. There he meets Jennifer Todd, victim of a drunken and abusive husband. Shortly after leaving the ranch, Roy discovers that his spare pistol is missing from his saddlebags. Knowing that Jennifer had taken it, and suspecting her purpose, Roy returns to the ranch. Jennifer is gone and there is a dead man in the ranch yard. Roy sets out in pursuit of Jennifer, and soon finds a pair of murderous hardcases on his own trail. The flight and pursuit lead Roy and Jennifer along the Devil's Highway to Yuma and thence up the Colorado River by steamboat. Well-paced and vivid action is spiced with the mystery caused by Jennifer's unexplained attitudes and behavior. Ample time is devoted to the developing relationship between Roy and Jennifer, as Roy struggles to reconcile his new feelings with the memories of his wife, and Jennifer deals with the reawakening of feelings deadened by life with her husband. Kirkus Reviews praised the author's "taut, stripped-down narration," and the book's combination of adventure and suspense with sympathetic characters resolving their problems in a believable way found favor with readers and reviewers.

The Gallows Land was followed in 1984 by a "Northern," *Starvation Camp* (Doubleday), much of which takes place in the Yukon Territory in the days of the Alaskan Gold Rush. Corporal Zachary McQuestion of the North-West Mounted

Police discovers the body of Mollie Malone, proprietor of a roadhouse in the Territory, murdered for her stock of food and whisky. In his pursuit of the killer, he survives a punishing wilderness trek, ambush, and snowslide. The trail then leads south to Seattle and thence to San Francisco and environs. The action is framed by authentic geographical and historical backgrounds, the result of the author's extensive but never obtrusive research. The ending opens the way for a sequel, which so far has not materialized.

Pronzini's Western detective character, John Quincannon, who is featured in the final story in the present collection, was introduced in *Quincannon* (Walker, 1985). He is an agent of the U.S. Secret Service, based in San Francisco in 1894. Pursuit of a gang of counterfeiters takes him to the rough Idaho mining town of Silver City, where theft, conspiracy, and murder are added to the counterfeiting. Like the protagonists of the previous two novels, Quincannon carries the weight of a tragic event from his past. In the cases of Roy Boone and Zack McQuestion, it is the loss of a loved one. For Quincannon, it is the result of a gun battle with criminals, in which a stray bullet from his gun killed a young pregnant woman and her unborn child; he has turned to alcohol in an attempt to drown the memory. In his pursuit of the villains he must contend with his bouts of drunkenness, and with the sometimes dubious help of the beautiful Sabina Carpenter, who is not what she pretends to be. At the end of the case, Quincannon resigns from the Secret Service and offers Sabina a partnership in a private detective agency, which she accepts (on a basis of "business only, of course").

Quincannon's second appearance was in *Beyond the Grave* (Walker, 1986), written with Marcia Muller. In this unusual collaboration, Quincannon investigates a case involving stolen religious artifacts, but is unable to resolve it completely.

Based on his written account of the case, Muller's modern-day detective Elena Oliverez is able to complete the solution.

In *The Last Days of Horse-Shy Halloran* (Evans, 1987), Pronzini shifts into a comic, if not manic, mode. The title character is Henry W. Halloran, a notorious if inept highwayman who, shall we say, does not deal well with horses (and vice versa). Halloran and his partner, the Wind River Kid, have come to the Montana town of Big Coulee to steal a shipment of gold. Opposing them are a Wells, Fargo detective, Sam Quarternight, and the Burgoyne Brothers, a rival band of robbers. There are robberies, jail-breaks, a kidnapping, thwarted love, and much to-ing and fro-ing, told in a style that maintains a delicate balance between straightforward adventure narrative and the tone of a nineteenth-century stage melodrama.

Pronzini's two most recent Western novels are *The Hangings* (Walker) and *Firewind* (Evans), both published in 1989 and both quite somber in content and tone. The former is an expanded version of the short story "The Hanging Man," included in this collection, with the setting transferred to a fictitious settlement in the section of northern California where Pronzini was born and raised. The latter also has a northern California setting: the rugged logging country between San Francisco and the Oregon border. It is a pure suspense novel about members of a small logging community who must flee a raging forest fire by train, only to find themselves faced with two additional menaces: a pair of ruthless killers, one of whom has a crippling terror of fire, and a highly flammable cargo of weapons, ammunition, and dynamite.

A fresh market for Western short fiction opened up in the 1980s: the hardcover or paperback anthology of new (non-reprint) stories. Four of the stories in the present collection are from such sources. Two other stories were written especially

INTRODUCTION

for this volume. In these stories the author finds his true Western voice. They do not depend on action or on the working out of a traditional Western plot. More often, they are stories of mood, atmosphere, and character, often told largely through dialogue or interior monologue: the kind of story a cowboy might tell at night around a campfire or in a lonely line-shack. When the author uses a standard Western figure or theme, it is usually for the purpose of confounding the reader's expectations by inverting the stereotype or cliché. Whether serious or comic, ironic or compassionate, the stories are authentic in detail and true in tone. There is surprisingly little overt violence, and no *casual* violence. When a violent act does occur, the impact is therefore all the greater.

The collection opens with "The Gambler," a story written for an anthology of original Western stories, *New Frontiers I* (Tor Books, 1990), edited by Pronzini and Martin H. Greenberg. It is a panorama of fifty years of Western history as seen through the eyes of a drifting gambler. The unnamed viewpoint character is more an observer than a participant in events, a fact reinforced by the unusual indirect narrative style, but through his recollections and reminiscences we gradually build up a portrait of the man and develop an emotional investment in his fate.

"Markers" is a brief, moody, ironic tale with a "twist" ending. It was written for the Western Writers of America anthology *Roundup* (Doubleday, 1982), edited by Stephen Overholser.

"Wooden Indian," which was first published in *Alfred Hitchcock's Mystery Magazine* in 1989, opens with the theft of a cigar-store indian and seems headed toward humor or quaintness, but the author turns this tale in quite another direction. The story's point is made gently through the warmth and down-to-earth attitude of the small-town sheriff who narrates it.

INTRODUCTION

The first of the originals is "Righteous Guns," in which the stereotypical characters, situations, and language of the traditional Western are put to deliberate and inventive use.

"Fergus O'Hara, Detective" began life as "The Riverboat Gold Robbery" in the March 1974 issue of *Alfred Hitchcock's Mystery Magazine*. It was expanded into the novel *Freebooty* (Bobbs-Merrill, 1976), published under the author's pseudonym "Jack Foxx." The current version is a revision of the original magazine novella with some elements from the novel incorporated. *Freebooty* was described in the publisher's jacket blurb as a "humorous historical formal mystery." With its background in riverboating and its setting in San Francisco during the Civil War it also qualifies as a Western, as does the short version presented here. Be assured, by the way, that reading the short version will not spoil the pleasures of the novel, a fine free-wheeling romp with a more elaborate crime plot, including two murders, and more overt humor, supplied by such ingredients as the unctuous Horace T. Goatleg and an insane parrot. It is one of the author's scarcer books, and well worth seeking out.

"All the Long Years" was written for the anthology *Westeryear* (M. Evans, 1988), edited by Ed Gorman. Once again a standard situation—a rancher tracking down a cow thief—turns in an unexpected direction, resulting in a strong and emotionally-charged story.

The earliest version of "Decision" was published under the title " 'I'll See to Your Horse' " in *Zane Grey Western Magazine* in 1971. That story was rewritten to form the opening of the novel *The Gallows Land*. The version included here is a composite of the two earlier ones, with the original ending only slightly altered.

A frontier setting lends itself naturally to the coming-of-age story, and this theme occurs frequently in Western fiction. "Cave of Ice," a collaboration with Marcia Muller, is a small-scale example, written for a "young adult" audience and published in *Boys' Life* in 1986. The unusual setting is based on an actual ice cave in Idaho which the authors visited. (Marcia Muller and Pronzini have collaborated on the editing of numerous anthologies of crime fiction, and one of Western fiction by women authors, *She Won the West*; on the massive critical survey *1001 Midnights: The Aficionado's Guide to Mystery and Detective Fiction*; and on three novels, including *Beyond the Grave*, mentioned earlier.)

It is possible for a story to have a Western atmosphere or "flavor" without making use of specific Western trappings. This is the case with "The Hanging Man," set in a small northern California town in the 1890s. This darkly atmospheric crime story appeared in *Ellery Queen's Mystery Magazine* for 12 August 1981, and has been reprinted several times since then. It was the basis for Pronzini's full-length novel, *The Hangings* (Walker, 1989).

"Hero," first published in Pronzini's collection of short-short crime stories, *Small Felonies* (St. Martin's, 1988), is an unsettling study of the lynch mentality in a mob and in an individual.

"McIntosh's Chute," set primarily in a logging camp in Oregon, describes a remarkable mechanism for transporting logs and how it figured in a case of rough frontier justice. The story appeared under the pseudonym Jack Foxx in *New Frontiers I*.

"Fyfe and the Drummers," the second of the new stories in this collection, is a humorous vignette built around an encounter between two patent-medicine salesmen in a Western barroom. One of the drummers is touting Dr. Wallmann's Celebrated Nerve and Brain Tonic, first mentioned in the novel *Quincannon* and obviously named after Pronzini's frequent collaborator, Jeffrey Wallmann.

John Quincannon, first a Secret Service agent and then a

INTRODUCTION

private detective in San Francisco in 1894, is clearly a spiritual relative of Fergus O'Hara. "No Room at the Inn" is the first Quincannon short story, written for the anthology *Crime at Christmas* (Thorsons: London, 1988) in response to editor Jack Adrian's request for "a Western Christmas mystery featuring Quincannon, with a mountain setting and lots of snow."

For the final selection in this book, Pronzini puts on his hat as historian and analyst of *genre* fiction and surveys the rise and fall of the pulp and digest-sized Western fiction magazines.

You have been delayed long enough in your exploration of this book. Sample the author's sharp character portraits, the evocations of a vanished way of life, the crime and detective stories in Western settings, the comic or ironic vignettes. All will amply repay your attention.

The Gambler

For most of his life, he said, nigh on fifty years, he'd been a sporting man.

Faro, that was his game, he said. He'd operated faro banks all over the West, been a mechanic in some of the fanciest gambling houses from one end of the frontier to the other. Poker? Sure, that too. He'd played poker and Brag for big stakes. Three-card monte and twenty-one and Pitch and just about any other card game you could name. His hands weren't much to look at now, all crippled up with arthritis like they were, but once, why he could hold one deck in the palm of his hand while he shuffled up another. That wasn't the least of what he could do, neither. He'd always been a square gambler . . . well, almost always, fella sometimes hit a losing streak and he had to eat then too, didn't he? Not that he'd ever worked any big-time gyps or cons, mind. Just every now and then held out an ace or stacked a deck whilst shuffling or reversed a cut—and done it in the company of men like Dick Clark and Frank Tarbeaux and Luke Short and the Earp brothers, with them watching with their hawk's eyes and never suspecting a thing. That was how good a mechanic *he* was in his prime.

Those had been wild times, he said, desperate times. But from soda to hock, they'd also been grand times. Oh Lordy, what grand times they had been!

Thing was, he hadn't set out to enter the Life. No, when he'd left Ohio for California that summer of '54, it had been gold-mining that was on his mind. Just sixteen that summer, all fixed to help work his brother John's claim in the Mother Lode. But when he got to Columbia, the gem of the southern mines, he'd found poor John a month dead of consumption and his claim sold off to pay debts—and *him* with just two dollars left out of his traveling money. Only job he could get was swamping at the Long Tom.

Hardly a man left now that remembers the Long Tom, he said, but in its day it was the swellest gambling house in Columbia, and Columbia itself the rip-snortin'est town in the whole of the Mother Lode. Thirty saloons, a stadium for bull and bear fights, close to a hundred and fifty faro banks . . . why there hadn't been a town like it since, except maybe Tombstone in the eighties. And that Long Tom, well, that Long Tom was so big it ran from one street clean through to another, with a doorway at either end. Twenty-four tables, twelve on each side of a center aisle wide as a stagecoach runway. Guards on both doors, two armed floormen, and when there was a ruckus those guards would draw their pistols and shoot out the big whale-oil lamps that hung over the aisle and then the doormen would lock the doors and the floormen would shine dark lanterns on the gents that were cheating or otherwise causing trouble and put an end to it, peaceable or unpeaceable. Then the floormen would rig up new lights and the games would commence again just as though nothing had happened.

Well, the Long Tom was owned by the Mitchell brothers, and what they did was, they rented out those twenty-four tables to professional gamblers like Charles Cora, who later on got himself hung for murder by the vigilantes in San Francisco, and Ad Pence and Governor Hobbs and John Milton Strain. Now John Milton Strain was a gold-hunter as well as a gambler, and he didn't mind taking a young buck along with him to do some of the hard labor. Also didn't mind teaching a young buck the ins and outs of the sporting trade. So that was how he'd learned cards, he said—from John Milton Strain, one of the best of the old-time card sharps. (Wasn't any slouch when it came to prospecting, neither, was John Milton. One day he found a gold nugget big as an adobe brick, ten inches wide and five inches thick—all high-grade ore that he melted down into a bar weighing more than thirty pounds. Sleeper's Gold Exchange paid him $7500 for that bar. $7500 for one bar of pure gold!)

He'd worked at the Long Tom three years, he said, learning the gambling trade from John Milton Strain . . . well enough finally so that he'd rented his own faro layout right alongside John Milton's. He might have stayed on longer, except that a fire burned the Long Tom down in '57—burned twelve square blocks of Columbia's business district along with it. The Mitchell brothers put up a new building, but John Milton had had his fill of Columbia by then and he decided he'd had his too. So the two of 'em set out together for greener pastures.

He'd spent nearly ten years touring the mining camps in California and Nevada, about half that time with John Milton Strain for a partner. During those years he learned to hold his own with just about anybody in a "hard cards" game for big stakes. Won more than he lost, consistent, and if it hadn't been for a fondness for hard spirits and the company of fast women, why he'd have been a rich man before he was thirty. Yes sir, a rich man. But money was made to be spent, that was his philosophy. The more he made, the hotter it got sitting there in his pockets; and when it commenced to burn holes, well, what was there to do then but take it out and spend it?

By early '66 he'd had enough of the mining camps; he craved a look at other parts of the frontier, a chance to play with the bigger names in the sporting trade. So he'd drifted east and north, he said, up to Montana and then down to Cheyenne, Wyoming, which was a wide-open town in those days. Plenty of sports there, all right, most of them with the "Hell-on-Wheels" crowd that was following the construction of the Union Pacific Railroad west from Omaha to Promontory Point, Utah.

Now along that Union Pacific route, he said, the railroad set up supply points and campgrounds for track workers and other laborers—impermanent tent-towns for thousands of men. Well, those railroaders played as hard as they worked, so it was only natural that the honky-tonkers would gravitate to the camps to oblige them. In Cheyenne, one of the few real towns along the route, he'd found scores of gamblers, square and sure-thing both, and dozens of small-timers working as ropers, cappers, and steerers. Madams and whores and pimps, too. And saloon operators and confidence men and dips and yeggs—the whole shebang. And what they'd do, every time the railroad moved its base of operations a little farther west, was to pack up *their* equipment and move right along with 'em. That was how the whole business came to be called Hell-on-Wheels.

He'd joined up with 'em in Cheyenne and stayed on through Fort Saunders and Laramie and Benton City. Crazy wild, those days were, he said. He'd teamed with Ornery Ed Meeker on a brace faro game, and in Fort Saunders he found out Meeker was holding out on him and they'd had it out and one Sunday afternoon he'd shot Meeker dead. Yes sir, one clean shot right in his whiskers. First man he'd ever killed, but not the last. Then he fell in with one of Eleanore Dumont's working girls, to his sorrow, for she stole three thousand dollars he'd won at faro and decamped with the money and a fellow named Peavey, one of Corn-Hole Johnny Gallagher's steerers.

Well, it was just crazy wild. And the wildest place of all was Benton City, which they came into the summer of '68. Hot? Lordy, it was hot that summer! North Platte River was two miles away and the water-haulers charged a dollar a barrel and

THE GAMBLER

ten cents a bucket; they had the best graft in town, by a damn sight. He'd worked the Empire Tent there, on account of it was the biggest operation and got the heaviest play and he figured he could make more than he could with his own box. Fellow who ran the Buffalo Hump Corral wanted him in there, too—offered him a piece of the action—but the Buffalo Hump specialized in a game called rondo coolo, which you played with a stick and ivory balls on a billiard table, and what did he know about a game like that? He was a card man, a faro dealer and poker sharp. That was what he knew and that was how he made his living.

He was working the Empire Tent when *he* got shot. Railroad worker accused him of marking cards, which he hadn't been, and hauled out a Colt's sixgun and put a slug in his left arm before he could bring his own weapon to bear. Well, he almost died. Almost lost his left arm and almost died, but if he *had* lost that arm he'd have wished he *had* died, he said, because how could a one-armed gambler expect to make out?

Took him three months to recover, and by then the Hell-on-Wheels bunch was getting ready to move on to the next stop. They left a hundred dead behind them, their own and railroaders both—a hundred in three months. And him with that busted wing and most of his cash gone for doctoring and whatnot. So he'd called it quits, right then and there. Hell-on-Wheels wasn't for him. Killed a man and almost been killed himself . . . no sir, that wasn't for him any more.

So he'd commenced to drifting again, building up stakes and losing 'em and building 'em back up again. Out to Kansas for a spell, Dodge City and the other cowtowns. Shot a man in the Long Branch in Dodge one day but the fellow didn't die; wasn't his fault that time neither, he said. Then, in '73, he'd got wind of a big silver strike in California, down in the Panamint Mountains, and of a new camp that had sprung up there called Panamint City.

Town was wide open when he got there, he said. They called it "a suburb of Hell," which he didn't think it was so far as sin was concerned, not after Hell-on-Wheels—but Lordy, it was *hot* as hell, up there above the floor of Death Valley like it was. Made the Wyoming plain seem like a cool riverside retreat.

First thing, he'd gone to work as a mechanic for Jim Bruce at the Dempsey and Boultinghouse Saloon. Now Bruce was a hardcase, having ridden the Missouri-Kansas border with Quantrill, and he didn't take kindly to insults and troublemakers. Another dealer, name of Bob McKenny, ran afoul of Bruce and tried to kill him, and what happened was, Jim Bruce blew his fool head off. And what did he do then, straightaway? Why, he took Bob McKenny right out and buried him, that's what he did, on account of Jim Bruce wasn't just a gambler, he was also Panamint City's undertaker!

Well, he said, after a year or so he started dealing for Dave Neagle at Dave's resort, the Oriental, which had a fancy black walnut bar and some of the spiciest paintings of the female form divine that a man ever set eyes on. He stayed on there for four years, and would have stayed longer, likely, for he and Dave Neagle got on fine and he'd taken up with one of the girls at Martha Camp's bawdy house, Sadie her name was, blond and plump like the women in the paintings over the Oriental's black walnut bar. But then a big rainstorm hit the Panamints and a flash flood came boiling down from the heights and swept up more than a hundred buildings as if they were bunches of sticks, the Oriental among 'em, and washed the wreckage all the way down Surprise Canyon and spread it over a mile of the Panamint Valley. Hadn't been for somebody up at one of the stamp mills spotting the flood and raising an alarm, he said, him and most of the other townspeople would have gone sailing down Surprise Canyon too.

From there he'd gone up to Bodie for a while, and then on back to Kansas and the queen of the cowtowns. But Dodge

THE GAMBLER

wasn't what she had been a decade earlier, he said, leastways not so far as a sporting man was concerned, and he hadn't stayed long—just long enough to get wind that Dick Clark and Lou Rickabaugh and Bill Harris, who had once owned the Long Branch, had gone into partnership and opened a resort out in Tombstone. Well, he'd never met Dick Clark and wished he had, for Clark was a legend among sporting men, so he'd set out for Arizona Territory. And when he arrived in Tombstone, why Dick Clark was every bit the gentleman he was reputed to be, and his Oriental Saloon and Gambling Hall at Allen and Fifth streets was by far the grandest gambling house in town. Fancy chandeliers and colored crystals set into the bar, which was finished in white and gilt, and a club room to knock the eye out of a Victorian swell . . . oh, it was grand! He'd never been in a grander place before nor since, he said.

Now Dick Clark, as befitted his station, had some mighty important gents dealing for him. He had Luke Short and Bat Masterson and Wyatt Earp and Doc Holliday, among others, and he paid them twenty-five dollars for a six-hour shift—princely wages for those times. That was where *he* wanted to work, no question about that, so he'd talked to Dick Clark and danged if Dick Clark hadn't hired him. And there he was, he said, dealing at the Oriental Saloon with Luke Short and Wyatt Earp and Doc Holliday and Bat Masterson, all of them swell fellows and don't let anybody tell you different.

Bat Masterson didn't stay long, having fish to fry elsewhere, but Wyatt and Doc, they stayed, and everybody knows what happened with them. Well, sure—they and Wyatt's brothers Virgil and Morgan got into a feud with the Clantons and the McLaury brothers and Curly Bill Brocius and John Ringo, and it all came to a head late in '81 when Morgan Earp got himself ambushed and then Wyatt went out in a vengeful rage and done for Curly Bill and a couple of others in the Clanton crowd. That was when they had the big shootout at the O.K. Corral. He was

there that day and he'd seen it all, he said. He'd seen the whole thing from soda to hock.
Nor was that all he'd seen that year, he said. He'd seen Luke Short gun down Charlie Storms, a hardcase who'd been one of the Hell-on-Wheels bunch. Happened right there in the Oriental, right smack in front of *his* table. It was Charlie Storms' doing, he said, no question about that, for he was a mean one and had been in several gunfights in Cheyenne and Deadwood and Leadville, and wanted to add an important name to his list of victims. But he met his match in Luke Short. He goaded little Luke, and goaded him some more, and then when push came to shove, why Luke outdrew him cool as you please and Charlie Storms died a surprised man.
Tombstone in the eighties was a fine place to be, he said, and he'd felt settled there, working for Dick Clark. Now and then he'd develop an itch, same as Dick Clark himself would, and get on a stagecoach and see what Lady Luck had in store in places like Tucson and Phoenix and Prescott and Las Vegas, New Mexico. But he never stayed long in any of those places—particularly not in Las Vegas, where he himself had been goaded into killing his second and last man, this time in a misunderstanding over a woman. He always went back to Tombstone and the Oriental Saloon and Gambling Hall. He was still dealing there, he said, when Dick Clark sold out his interest in '94 and retired from the Life.
He was likewise of retirement age by then, but unlike Dick Clark and some of the other old-timers who'd made their fortunes and bought houses and saloons and other property, or invested their money in stocks and bonds and such, and were comfortably fixed for the rest of their days, *he* was still just a mechanic. Flush some of the time, broke more often. Never saved any of his winnings, never invested any of it or bought any property other than what he could carry in a pair of

carpetbags. Sport like him couldn't afford to retire. All he could do, he said, was keep right on dealing cards.

So after Dick Clark sold out his interest in the Oriental, he'd gone on down to Bisbee, which was still a fair hot town in the mid-nineties, and worked for a time in Cobweb Hall. Then he'd moved on to Phoenix and Prescott, and then up to Virginia City, Nevada, and then over to Albuquerque. He was in Albuquerque when the new century came in, he said, sixty-two years old and stony broke in Albuquerque, New Mexico. But then he'd won a stake and moved on to Taos, and then over into Texas—San Antonio and El Paso and Austin and Tascosa—and then back into Arizona Territory, to see if Tombstone was anything like it had been in the old days. But it wasn't. No sir, *none* of the towns were like they'd been in the old days. They were all changed, and still changing so fast you could almost see it happening right before your eyes.

Once, he said, the sporting man had commanded respect. Not just the high-rollers like Dick Clark, no, ordinary sports like himself. Why, you could walk down the street in just about any town and gents would doff their hats and smile and wish you good day. Women would smile, too, some of them, and more than you'd think would do more than smile. Oh, you were somebody in those days, he said. You had a skill few had, and you made big money, and you were somebody and you had respect.

But not after the new century came in. Not after all the people moved west and shrank the land and tamed it. Everything changed then. Men quit smiling and doffing their hats and wishing you good day. Women wouldn't have anything to do with you, none except the whores. They all whispered behind your back and gave you dirty looks and shunned you like you were a common thief. And then the territorial leaders that wanted statehood, they went and put those laws in, all those antigambling laws. Blamed gambling and sporting men for society's ills and took away their livelihood and made them outlaws and outcasts.

It wasn't fair, he said, it wasn't right. What could men like him do, men who'd been in the Life for nigh on fifty years? Where could they go? Some took to running illegal games, sure, but those were the young ones. What about the ones past their prime, old men with hands starting to cripple with arthritis? What about them?

Memories, that was all they left him. Fifty years of memories . . . all the places he'd been, all the things he'd seen and done, all the men and women he'd known. He'd seen it all in those fifty years, by grab. He'd *lived* it all. Been a part of the wildness, and of the slow taming too. But now . . . now the land was too tame, it was like a tiger that had become a pussycat. This wasn't the frontier anymore, a place with growl and howl; this was just a tamed tiger meowing in the sun.

Well, *he* remembered the old days, he said. *He* knew how wild and desperate those times had been. And how grand, too. Oh Lordy, what grand times they had been!

They found him one morning in the dust behind Simpson's Barber Shop, lying crumpled in the dust with his nightshirt pulled up to expose the swollen veins in his pipestem legs. He must have come out during the night to use the outhouse, the town marshal said. Left his room at the rear of the shop, where Simpson had let him live in exchange for sweeping up, and set out for the privy and had a seizure before he got there. He hadn't died right away, though. He'd crawled a ways, ten feet or so toward the privy; the marks were plain in the dust.

That afternoon, the undertaker and his assistant put the corpse in a plain pine box, loaded the box into the mortuary wagon, and drove up the hill to the cemetery. The only other citizen to go along with them was the preacher, but he didn't tarry long. The old man hadn't been religious and had never attended church services; it was only out of common decency that the preacher had decided to speak a few words over the grave. Besides, it was hot that day. Hot as the hinges of hell, the preacher said just before he rode his horse back down the hill.

The undertaker and his assistant made short work of the burying and laid their tools in the wagon. The assistant mopped his sweating face with his handkerchief, spoke then for the first time since their arrival.

"You think he *was* a sporting man?"

"That old coot?" the undertaker said. "Now what makes you ask that?"

"Well, all those stories he would tell . . ."

"Stories, that's all they were. Old man's imaginings. He had nothing when he come here and nothing when he died. No money, no kin, no friends to speak of—nobody, even, to buy him a marker for his final resting place. And him supposed to have been a fancy card sharp rubbing elbows with Wyatt Earp and Bat Masterson? Pshaw!"

The undertaker shook his head, turned to look down the dry brown hill at the dry brown town crouching in the summer heat; at the desert beyond, rolling away like a dead sea toward the horizon.

"Wasn't nobody at all," he said.

Markers

J ACK BOHANNON and I had been best friends for close to a year, ever since he'd hired on at the Two Bar Cross, but if it hadn't been for a summer squall that came up while the two of us were riding fence, I'd never have found out about who and what he was. Or about the markers.

We'd been out two weeks, working the range southeast of Eagle Mountain. The fences down along there were in middling fair shape, considering the winter we'd had; Bohannon and I sported calluses from the wire cutters and stretchers, but truth to tell, we hadn't been exactly overworking ourselves. Just kind of moving along at an easy pace. The weather had been fine—cool crisp mornings, warm afternoons, sky scrubbed clean of clouds on most days—and it made you feel good just to be there in all that sweet-smelling open space.

As it happened, we were about two miles east of the Eagle Mountain line shack when the squall came up. Came up fast, too, along about three o'clock in the afternoon, the way a summer storm does sometimes in Wyoming Territory. We'd been planning to spend a night at the line shack anyway, to replenish our supplies, so as soon as the sky turned cloudy dark we lit a shuck straight for it. The rain started before we were halfway there, and by the time we raised the shack, the downpour was such that you couldn't see a dozen rods in front of you. We were both soaked in spite of our slickers; rain like that has a way of slanting in under any slicker that was ever made.

The shack was just a one-room sod building with walls coated in ashes-and-clay and a whipsawed wood floor. All that was in it was a pair of bunks, a table and two chairs, a larder, and a big stone fireplace. First things we did when we came inside, after sheltering the horses for the night in the lean-to out back, were to build a fire on the hearth and raid the larder. Then, while we dried off, we brewed up some coffee and cooked a pot of beans and salt pork. It was full dark by then and that storm was kicking up a hell of a fuss; you could see lightning blazes outside the single window, and hear thunder grumbling in the distance and the wind moaning in the chimney flue.

When we finished supper Bohannon pulled a chair over in front of the fire, and I sat on one of the bunks, and we took out the makings. Neither of us said much at first. We didn't have to talk to enjoy each other's company; we'd spent a fair lot of time together in the past year—working the ranch, fishing and hunting, a little mild carousing in Saddle River—and we had an easy kind of friendship. Bohannon had never spoken much about himself, his background, his people, but that was all right by me. Way I figured it, every man was entitled to as much privacy as he wanted.

But that storm made us both restless; it was the kind of night a man sooner or later feels like talking. And puts him in a mood to share confidences, too. Inside a half hour we were swapping stories, mostly about places we'd been and things we'd done and seen.

That was how we came to the subject of markers—grave markers, first off—with me the one who brought it up. I was telling about the time I'd spent a year prospecting for gold in the California Mother Lode, before I came back home to Wyoming Territory and turned to ranch work, and I recollected the grave I'd happened on one afternoon in a rocky meadow south of Sonora. A mound of rocks, it was, with a wooden marker anchored at the north end. And on the marker was an epitaph scratched out with a knife.

"I don't know who done it," I said, "or how come that grave was out where it was, but that marker sure did make me curious. Still does. What it said was, 'Last resting place of I. R. Lyon. Lived and died according to his name.'"

I'd told that story a time or two before and it had always brought a chuckle, if not a horse laugh. But Bohannon didn't chuckle. Didn't say anything, either. He just sat looking into the fire, not moving, a quirly drifting smoke from one corner of his mouth. He appeared to be studying on something inside his head.

I said, "Well, *I* thought it was a mighty unusual marker, anyhow."

Bohannon still didn't say anything. Another ten seconds or so passed before he stirred—took a last drag off his quirly and tossed it into the fire.

"I saw an unusual marker myself once," he said then, quiet. His voice sounded different than I'd ever heard it.

"Where was that?"

"Nevada. Graveyard in Virginia City, about five years ago."

"What'd it say?"

"Said 'Here lies Adam Bricker. Died of hunger in Virginia City, August 1882.'"

"Hell. How could a man die of hunger in a town?"

"That's what I wanted to know. So I asked around to find out."

"Did you?"

"I did," Bohannon said. "According to the local law, Adam Bricker'd been killed in a fight over a woman. Stabbed by the woman's husband, man named Greenbaugh. Supposed to've been self-defense."

"If Bricker was stabbed, how could he have died of hunger?"

"Greenbaugh put that marker on Bricker's grave. His idea of humor, I reckon. Hunger Bricker died of wasn't hunger for food, it was hunger for the woman. Or so Greenbaugh claimed."

"Wasn't it the truth?"

"Folks I talked to didn't think so," Bohannon said. "Story was, Bricker admired Greenbaugh's wife and courted her some; she and Greenbaugh weren't living together and there was talk of a divorce. Nobody thought he trifled with her, though. That wasn't Bricker's way. Folks said the real reason Greenbaugh killed him was because of money Bricker owed him. Bricker's claim was that he'd been cheated out of it, so he refused to pay when Greenbaugh called in his marker. They had an argument, there was pushing and shoving, and when Bricker drew a gun and tried to shoot him, Greenbaugh used his knife. That was his story, at least. Only witness just happened to be a friend of his."

"Who was this Greenbaugh?"

"Gambler," Bohannon said. "Fancy man. Word was he'd cheated other men at cards, and debauched a woman or two—that was why his wife left him—but nobody ever accused him to his face except Adam Bricker. Town left him pretty much alone."

"Sounds like a prize son of a bitch," I said.

"He was."

"Men like that never get what's coming to them, seems like."

"This one did."

"You mean somebody cashed in his chips for him?"

"That's right," Bohannon said. "Me."

I leaned forward a little. He was looking into the fire, with his head cocked to one side, like he was listening for another rumble of thunder. It seemed too quiet in there, of a sudden, so I cleared my throat and smacked a hand against my thigh.

I said, "How'd it happen? He cheat you at cards?"
"He didn't have the chance."
"Then how . . . ?"
Bohannon was silent again. One of the burning logs slid off the grate and made a sharp cracking sound; the noise seemed to jerk him into talking again. He said, "There was a vacant lot a few doors down from the saloon where he spent most of his time. I waited in there one night, late, and when he came along, on his way to his room at one of the hotels, I stepped out and put my gun up to his head. And I shot him."
"My God," I said. "You mean you *murdered* him?"
"You could call it that."
"But damn it, man, why?"
"He owed me a debt. So I called in his marker."
"What debt?"
"Adam Bricker's life."
"I don't see—"
"I didn't tell you how I happened to be in Virginia City. Or how I happened to visit the graveyard. The reason was Adam Bricker. Word reached me that he was dead, but not how it happened, and I went there to find out."
"Why? What was Bricker to you?"
"My brother," he said. "My real name is Jack Bricker."
I got up off the bunk and went to the table and turned the lamp up a little. Then I got out my sack of Bull Durham, commenced to build another smoke. Bohannon didn't look at me; he was still staring into the fire.
When I had my quirly lit I said, "What'd you do after you shot Greenbaugh?"
"Got on my horse and rode out of there."
"You figure the law knows you did it?"
"Maybe. But the law doesn't worry me much."
"Then how come you changed your name? How come you traveled all the way up here from Nevada?"

"Greenbaugh had a brother, too," he said. "Just like Adam had me. He was living in Virginia City at the time and he knows I shot Greenbaugh. I've heard more than once that he's looking for me—been looking ever since it happened."

"So he can shoot you like you shot his brother?"

"That's right. I owe him a debt, Harv, same as Greenbaugh owed me one. One of these days he's going to find me, and when he does he'll call in his marker, same as I did mine."

"Maybe he won't find you," I said. "Maybe he's stopped looking by this time."

"He hasn't stopped looking. He'll never stop looking. He's a hardcase like his brother was."

"That don't mean he'll ever cross your trail—"

"No. But he will. It's just a matter of time."

"What makes you so all-fired sure?"

"A feeling I got," he said. "Had it ever since I heard he was after me."

"Guilt," I said, quiet.

"Maybe. I'm not a killer, not truly, and I've had some bad nights over Greenbaugh. But it's more than that. It's something I know is going to happen, like knowing the rain will stop tonight or tomorrow and we'll have clear weather again. Maybe because there are too many markers involved, if you take my meaning—the grave kind and the debt kind. One of these days I'll be dead because I owe a marker."

Neither of us had anything more to say that night. Bohannon—I couldn't seem to think of him as Bricker—got up from in front of the fire and climbed into his bunk, and when I finished my smoke I did the same. What he'd told me kept rattling around inside my head. It was some while before I finally got to sleep.

I woke up right after dawn, like I always do—and there was Bohannon, with his saddlebags packed and his bedroll under one arm, halfway to the door. Beyond him, through the window, I could see pale gray light and enough of the sky to make out broken clouds; the storm had passed.

"What the hell, Bohannon?"

"Time for me to move on," he said.

"Just like that? Without notice to anybody?"

"I reckon it's best that way," he said. "A year in one place is long enough—maybe too long. I was fixing to leave anyway, after you and me finished riding fence. That's why I went ahead and told you about my brother and Greenbaugh and the markers. Wouldn't have if I'd been thinking on staying."

I swung my feet off the bunk and reached for my Levi's. "It don't make any difference to me," I said. "Knowing what you done, I mean."

"Sure it does, Harv. Hell, why lie to each other about it?"

"All right. But where'll you go?"

He shrugged. "Don't know. Somewhere. Best if you don't know, best if I don't myself."

"Listen, Bohannon—"

"Nothing to listen to." He came over and put out his hand, and I took it, and there was the kind of feeling inside me I'd had as a button when a friend died of the whooping cough. "Been good knowing you, Harv," he said. "I hope you don't come across a marker someday with my name on it." And he was gone before I finished buttoning up my pants.

From the window I watched him saddle his horse. I didn't go outside to say a final word to him—there wasn't anything more to say; he'd been right about that—and he didn't look back when he rode out. I never saw him again.

But that's not the whole story, not by any means.

Two years went by without me hearing anything at all about Bohannon. Then Curly Polk, who'd worked with the two of us on the Two Bar Cross and then gone down to Texas for a while, drifted back our way for the spring roundup, and he brought word that Bohannon was dead. Shot six weeks earlier, in the Pecos River town of Santa Rosa, New Mexico.

But it hadn't been anybody named Greenbaugh who pulled the trigger on him. It had been a local cowpuncher, liquored up, spoiling for trouble; and it had happened over a spilled drink that Bohannon had refused to pay for. The only reason Curly found out about it was that he happened to pass through Santa Rosa on the very day they hung the puncher for his crime.

It shook me some when Curly told about it. Not because Bohannon was dead—too much time had passed for that—but because of the circumstances of his death. He'd believed, and believed hard, that someday he'd pay for killing Greenbaugh; that there were too many markers in his life and someday he'd die on account of one he owed. Well, he'd been wrong. And yet the strange thing, the pure crazy thing, was that he'd also been right.

The name of the puncher who'd shot him was Sam Marker.

Wooden Indian

I WAS LAYING a fire in the cast-iron stove when Henry Bandelier, who owns the Elk Basin General Merchandise Store, came rushing into my office. Usually Bandelier is the unflappable sort, but he was in a dither this cold October morning; he was so flappable, in fact, with his feet moving and his arms sawing up and down, he looked like a scrawny pink crow about to take flight.

"Sheriff, I been robbed!"

That brought me right up to attention. I didn't much care for Bandelier—he was a loudmouth, and no more honest than he had to be—but you don't have to care for a man to do your duty by him.

"The hell you say. When did it happen?"

"Middle of the night," he said.

"How much is missing?"

"How much? *All* of it, of course!"

"All the money in your cashbox?"

"Money? Who said anything about money?"

"Well, you did . . . didn't you?"

"No! Wasn't money that was stolen. It was my indian."

". . . Come again?"

"You heard me, Sheriff. My prize wooden indian's been pilfered."

"Now who in tarnation would steal that monstros—" I stopped, cleared my throat, and started over. "That indian's been setting out in front of your store six or seven years now. Weighs two hundred pounds if it weighs an ounce. Who'd want to go and steal it?"

"Tom Black Wolf, that's who."

"Oh, now . . ."

"It's a fact," Bandelier said. "You can't go sticking up for that boy this time, Lucas Monk. Him and that cousin of his, Charlie Walks Far, stole my indian in the dead of night and that's the plain truth."

"How do you know it was them?"

"Lloyd Cooper told me so, that's how I know. He was awake at three A.M., using his chamberpot, and he heard a wagon rattling by the hotel and looked out and it was Tom Black Wolf and Charlie Walks Far making off with my indian."

"How could Lloyd tell who was on the wagon, at that distance?"

"There was a moon last night," Bandelier said. "You know that as well as I do. A big fat harvest moon. Lloyd saw them plain. Saw something eight feet long in the bed, too, under a piece of canvas. Said it looked like a body. Ain't anything eight feet long that looks like a covered-up corpse, by God, except my indian."

That was open to debate, but trying to argue with a fractious Henry Bandelier was like trying to argue with a mean-spirited bull in rutting season. I said, "All right, Mr. Bandelier. You just simmer down. I'll drive out to the reservation and have a talk with Tom Black Wolf."

"Talk with him, hell. You arrest him, Sheriff, you hear me? You arrest him and bring back my indian or I'll know the reason why!" He turned on his heel and stalked out.

I stood puzzling for a time in the cold office. *The reason why.* Well, that was the question uppermost in my mind, even if it wasn't uppermost in Henry Bandelier's.

WOODEN INDIAN

What would a couple of Indians want with an eight-foot, two-hundred pound wooden indian?

The damn Model T wouldn't start without I spent twenty minutes at the crank, aggravating my bursitis with every turn. Contraption never failed to give me trouble as soon as the weather turned frosty. Come the winter snows, I'd lock it in my barn again and leave it there until the thaw. Progress is all well and good, and in 1915 a county sheriff's got to have a modern conveyance or folks don't think he's serious about his job; but if you ask me, a good horse is a better asset to a man than any motor car ever manufactured. Horses don't freeze up in the winter, for one thing. And you don't have to crank one until your arm pretty near falls off to get it started on cold mornings.

I pedaled the flivver into low gear and drove on down Main Street, with the exhaust farting smoke and sparks all the way. The front of Henry Bandelier's store looked some better without that wooden indian rearing up next to the entrance. Most folks in Elk Basin would agree with that, too; Bandelier had had more than one complaint about it over the years. But he was right paternal about that indian, which was ironical because he didn't like real Indians at all; he'd trade with the ones on the reservation but he made them come around to the rear so as not to "offend" his white customers. He claimed the wooden indian had been a gift from the Cuba Libre Cigar Company of Cleveland, Ohio, in honor of the fact that he sold more Cuba Libre crooks and panatelas than any other merchant in the state. More likely, he'd made some kind of deal with the Cuba Libre people to display that indian, which had their name written across the chest in bold red letters, in exchange for a fatter discount. Either way, it was an eyesore. And not just on account of its size. It was rough-carved of some tobacco-spit brown wood, the limbs and head were all out of proportion to the body, a piece of the nose had been shot off by a drunken cowboy one Fourth of July, and the "cigars" it was clutching were so big and phallic-looking they'd caused more than one woman to blush when Bandelier first unveiled it.

Officially, though, that wooden indian might have been the Mona Lisa: it was stolen property, its theft a felony offense. The law's the law and I'm sworn to uphold it. But it sure would pain me to have to arrest Tom Black Wolf and Charlie Walks Far for the crime. Especially young Tom.

He was twenty-two, smart as a whip, and down-deep honest. You could trust him with your money and likely your life, which is a hell of a lot more than I'd say for most white men in Elk Basin. He'd whizzed through agency school, and at the urging of Abe Fetters, the Indian agent, and Doc Cranston and me and a couple of others, he'd come in to attend high school right here in town. Graduated at the top of his class, too. He wanted to be an agronomist. I had to go look that up. It means somebody who specializes in field-crop production and soil management, which is to say somebody who can make crops grow on poor land. He'd applied to the state university and been accepted and would have enrolled last semester—he'd been working two jobs off the reservation to save up enough for his tuition—except that his grandfather, old Chief Victor, had taken mortal sick. Tom idolized Chief Victor, who had once been a great warrior and who was descended from and named after the head chief of the Flatheads during the middle of the last century; and he just wouldn't leave the reservation while the old man was on his death bed. Well, Chief Victor had been on his death bed three months now and was likely to lie there another three before he finally let go. These old warriors die hard.

So that was Tom Black Wolf. And Charlie Walks Far was all right, too. Not as bright as Tom, but a hard-worker and no trouble to anybody. It just didn't make sense that those two, of all the people in the county, red or white, would have swiped

WOODEN INDIAN

Bandelier's damned cigar company indian. Not even as a prank; they were too sober-sided for that sort of foolishness.

It was a dozen miles out to the reservation, along a road that had been built for wagons, not Model T Fords. The motor car was contrary at the best of times; on such a road as this it kept bucking and lurching, as if it didn't like my company or my hands on its steering wheel. By the time I drove onto reservation land, my backside was sorer than if I'd been sitting a saddle twenty-four hours straight.

The reservation was poor land, rocky and hilly, with almost no decent bottomland. No wonder Tom Black Wolf wanted to be an agronomist; you'd have to have special training, and maybe divine help, to grow worthwhile crops in soil like this. That was the federal government for you: force the Indians onto such land and then expect them to lick your boots in gratitude just because the land was free. It was a hell of a thing to be born with a skin color different than the men who ran the country, particularly when the country had been yours in the first place.

Close to five hundred Indians lived there—Flatheads, mostly, with a few Piegans and Bloods. Their homes were slab-built shacks put up by the government back in the Seventies, most of them scattered around a small, shallow lake. There were some ramshackle barns and livestock pens—the Indians ran sheep, goats, and a few head of cattle—and an agency store and an infirmary where the poorly trained reservation doctor treated ills and disease with such medicines as the Bureau of Indian Affairs doled out. Tweaked my conscience every time I came out here, even though I'd had nothing to do with building the place or with running it. It was squalor, plain and simple, two generations' worth, and no man worth his salt faces squalor with a clear conscience.

A dirt road rimmed the lake, and the flivver made so much noise rattling along it that kids and dogs ran and hid. When I came up to Chief Victor's house—bigger than most, as befitted his station—Tom Black Wolf appeared in the doorway. He watched me shut the motor down and climb off and walk on over to him. Usually he had a smile for me, but today he was all Indian; there wasn't any more expression on his lean face or in his eyes than there was in Henry Bandelier's wooden indian.

I didn't smile either. I said, "Morning, Tom. Taste of snow in the air, wouldn't you say?"

"Yes. Have you come to see me, Sheriff Lucas?"

"Some questions I'd like to ask you. I don't want to disturb your grandfather, though. We can talk out here."

"Chief Victor has been moved to the infirmary. The doctor requested it two days ago."

"He's bad off, then?"

"Yes. It is almost his time."

"I'm sorry, Tom."

"You shouldn't be," he said. "It is only a passage. Chief Victor has led a long and honorable life and he will find his reward." I nodded, and Tom said then, formal, "Please come inside where it's warm."

We went in. Tom kept the place clean, and mostly neat except for books. He was a reader, Tom was—read anything and everything, on just about any subject you could name. Hungry for knowledge, that was Tom Black Wolf. There were books on the wood-block tables and chairs and scattered in piles over the painted board floor. Some were his, that he'd bought through mail-order; others belonged to the new Elk Basin Lending Library. Miss Mary Ellen Belknap, the librarian and town historian, let him check out as many as he wanted, despite the few good citizens who frowned on such generosity.

I went over and stood by the stove, to thaw myself out. Tom let me warm some before he said, "You have questions, you said?"

"It's a law matter. Seems that wooden indian sets out in front of Henry Bandelier's store was stolen last night. He thinks you and Charlie Walks Far did the deed."

Tom didn't say anything.

"Did you, son? You and Charlie?"

He just looked at me with his face set and his lips pressed tight together. That gave me another twinge, for it told me he was guilty, all right, and that he wasn't going to own up to it. An Indian who respects you—and I knew Tom respected me—won't lie to your face, the way a white man will. Instead he keeps his mouth shut and lets you think whatever you like.

"Tom," I said, "stealing's a serious crime, you know that. Even if it is of a public eyesore. If you've got that wooden indian around here somewhere, I'll find it. Go easier on you and Charlie if you tell me where it is and your reason for making off with it."

"You're welcome to search, Sheriff Lucas."

"Is that all you got to say?"

He nodded. Once.

"All right, then," I said. "I'll just go ahead and see what's what around here."

Which I did, and of course I didn't find any sign of that eight-foot hunk of wood. Finding it wasn't going to be *that* easy. When I was done I walked with him to the flivver, and then stopped and turned and said, "You been doing some saw work this morning, Tom?"

It didn't faze him. Takes a better white man than me to surprise an Indian, I guess. He said, bland as you please, "Saw work?"

"Got sawdust all over your shoes." He did, too; I'd noticed it while I was warming up at the stove. "Don't look like cottonwood or jackpine or any other wood grows around here. Matter of fact, it looks like that tobacco-spit brown wood Henry Bandelier's statue is carved out of."

Tom didn't say anything.

"Cut it up for firewood, did you?"

Silence.

"Or maybe it offended you boys somehow. That it?"

Silence.

I sighed, though not so's he could hear me do it, and said, "Reckon I'll be back, Tom," and got into the flivver.

I found Charlie Walks Far tending sheep on the hardscrabble land north of the lake. I had to leave the Ford on the road; if I'd tried to drive up to where Charlie was, I'd have busted an axle or bruised my liver or both. But I was just wasting my time. Charlie was as close-mouthed as Tom. No lies, no admissions; just civility and nothing more.

So then I went to see Abe Fetters, the Indian agent who also ran the reservation store. He didn't know anything about the wooden indian—not that I expected him to—and said he just couldn't believe Tom Black Wolf and Charlie Walks Far would resort to common thievery.

"Particularly not now," Abe went on, "with Chief Victor so sick. Why, it'd be an act of disrespect, and you know how Tom idolizes his grandfather."

"Maybe they had a good reason for it," I said.

"They may have thought so. But what?"

"Well, I don't know. Some ceremonial reason, maybe?"

Abe laughed without much humor. "Take my word for it," he said, "there's no Flathead ceremony involving a wooden indian."

I asked him to help me comb the village and see what we could find. He said he would. And we did. And that was another big waste of time. Whatever Tom and Charlie had done with the statue, it was well hidden—or its remains were. We didn't find even a speck of sawdust to match the kind on Tom's shoes.

We stopped finally at the infirmary, for I thought it proper to pay my respects—likely my last respects—to Chief Victor. But the old man was asleep and the halfbreed doctor, Joshua Teel, wouldn't let me in to see him. Chief Victor likely wouldn't recognize me anyway, Teel said; the old warrior was mostly delirious now and had been for a couple of days.

So it was a morning of frustrations all around.

Wasn't anything for me to do then but drive on back to Elk Basin. It was well past noon by that time, and I was almost as hungry as I was puzzled. None of it made a lick of sense. Hell, if anything the theft made less sense now than it had before I'd visited the reservation.

Why would two basically honest young Indians steal a worthless wooden indian? And why in tarnation would they take a saw to it once they had it?

Back in town I put the Model T away in the City Hall barn and then went and hunted up Lloyd Cooper and had a little talk with him. After which I took my sore bones to the Elite Cafe for a late lunch. But before I could eat it, Henry Bandelier came prancing in; he'd seen me drive through earlier and he'd also seen that I was alone—no Tom Black Wolf, no Charlie Walks Far, and no wooden indian.

"Well?" he demanded, after he'd sat down uninvited at my table. "Why didn't you arrest those two bucks?"

"I didn't arrest 'em," I said, "on account of I got no evidence they're the guilty parties."

"No evidence? Hogwash! I told you Lloyd Cooper saw them stealing my indian in the middle of the night."

"That's not exactly what Lloyd saw. I just talked to him myself a few minutes ago. He saw Tom and Charlie, all right, on board a wagon with something in the bed under a piece of canvas, but he didn't see what that something was. Not so much as a glimpse of it."

"It was my indian. You know it was!"

"I don't know any such thing," I said. "I didn't find that statue of yours out at the reservation, nor anybody who knew anything about it."

Bandelier shaped his lips like a man about to spit. "Just how carefully did you search, Sheriff?"

"Carefully enough." I fixed him with a hard eye. "And I don't like your tone, Mr. Bandelier. You implying that I haven't done my duty?"

"If the shoe fits," he said, prissy.

"Well, it don't fit," I said. "Now suppose you take yourself back behind your store counter and let me eat my lunch in peace and quiet."

"I'm warning you, Sheriff Monk . . ."

"You're doing what?"

He didn't like what he saw in my face. He scraped back his chair, not meeting my eyes now, and said to my left shoulder, "If you won't do anything about those two thieving Flatheads, then I will."

"Such as?"

"That's my business."

"Not if it involves breaking the law. You do anything illegal, like going out to the reservation yourself with mischief in mind, and I'll cloud up and rain all over you. And you can damned well count on that."

I spoke loud, so that the five other citizens in the Elite could also hear my words plain. Bandelier's face got even redder than it already was. But he didn't sling any more words of his own; he put his back to me and walked out all stiff and righteous, like a sinner leaving a tent meeting.

Well, hell, I thought.

Now I'd lost my appetite.

Henry Bandelier was born without the sense God gave a picket-pin gopher: He tried to stir up trouble in spite of my warning. He talked long and fast to anybody who'd listen about the "red heathens out on the reservation," and what lowdown thieves they were, and even though it had been years since we'd had any problems to speak of with the Indians, there were some hotheads who believed him. There'd have been an incident come out of it, too, with white men and red both getting hurt, if I hadn't got wind of a midnight meeting in the back of Bandelier's store. Half a dozen men were there, armed with ax handles and fortified with free liquor, and they were getting ready to ride on out to the reservation to "teach those Indians a lesson," as Bandelier was saying, when I busted in.

I chased the others home and threw Bandelier in jail on a charge of inciting to riot. He squawked long and loud, which was fine with me; he also made some thinly veiled threats, which wasn't fine with me. So I added "threatening a peace officer with bodily harm" to the charges against him.

In the morning Bandelier demanded his lawyer. When Jack Dunlap showed up I talked to him first, after which he consulted with Bandelier in private for the better part of an hour. What he said must have put the fear of God into the storekeeper; Bandelier was some subdued when we all went trooping over to see Judge Cooney. The judge let Bandelier out on bail, and I promised to reduce the charges against him on the proviso that he quit trying to provoke conflict with the Indians and leave the matter of the missing statue in the hands of the law.

That put an end to the trouble. Bandelier had too much self-esteem to suffer a public disgrace lightly; he retreated into his store and his humiliation, and from then on kept his big mouth shut.

I continued to investigate the theft, off and on for two days, but there just wasn't anything to find out. I was considering another drive out to the reservation when Abe Fetters showed up in town with the news that Chief Victor had died.

I talked to Abe over at the train depot, where he was picking up a consignment of supplies from the government. He said the old man had passed on two nights ago, in his sleep. Yesterday there'd been the usual tribal ceremony presided over by the medicine man. Today, though, there'd been something that *wasn't* usual.

"What's that, Abe?" I asked.

"Well, the burial," he said. "They took his remains out to the burial ground before dawn without telling the medicine man. Or me, for that matter. I didn't find out until after it was already done."

"Who did?"

"Tom Black Wolf and members of his family. Funny breach of custom. First time anything like it has happened."

"Tom give you an explanation?"

"No," Abe said. "I asked him and so did the medicine man, but he wouldn't say. He must have had a good reason, though. Indians don't do anything without a good reason."

"You got any idea what it might be?"

"Not a one."

Neither did I, right then.

But I sure did that evening.

The official part of my day ends at six o'clock, when my night deputy, Gus Beemis, comes on. Since I lost my wife Tess two years ago, my evenings tend to be pretty quiet and of a sameness. Usually I have supper at the Elite Cafe, go on home, do such chores as need doing, turn in, and read myself to sleep. Gets lonely sometimes, especially around the holidays, but a man learns to live with that, same as he learns to live with all the other things, good and bad, that make up his life.

Some evenings after supper I stop by the library before I head home, to pick up and return books. In my early days I wasn't much of a reader; but after Tess passed on I took it up on a regular basis, just as Tom Black Wolf had, and found that I'd been short-changing myself most of my life. Books are more than just tools of knowledge; good books are friends. Better friends, some of them, than the human variety.

This was one of my nights to stop by the library. And I chanced to walk in while Mary Ellen Belknap was having a conversation with Lydia Cranston, Doc Cranston's wife. Indians was what they were talking about—Chief Victor's passing, at first. The library is small, so I couldn't have helped overhearing them if I'd wanted to. And I didn't want to when their talk shifted to Tom Black Wolf.

"I swan," Mary Ellen said, "I'll never understand Indians."

"Why do you say that?" Lydia asked.

"Well, you take Tom Black Wolf. He's always been such a good boy. Smart, well-mannered, and respectful of property. That's why I've let him check out books since he was in high school; he never abused the privilege. But now . . . well, I hope he isn't going to start running wild."

"Why would you think he'd start running wild, for heaven's sake?"

"It's the little things, isn't it?" Mary Ellen said. "That's how it always starts. And now that Chief Victor is gone, the authority figure in Tom's life—"

"*What* little things?"

"The last batch of books he checked out were overdue for almost two weeks. He's never had overdue books before."

"Well, my land, with his grandfather so sick—"

"That's not all," Mary Ellen said. "He also mutilated a book."

"He did what?"

"Mutilated a book. Don't look at me that way, Lydia, it's true. He tore a photograph out of an expensive history book.

Oh, he pasted it back in but you can see plainly where it was ripped out—"

I was over at the desk by then. I said, "Mary Ellen, when did you find out about this torn photograph?"

She blinked at me. She's six feet tall and horse-faced and when she blinks she looks like a startled mare. "Why . . . just this afternoon, Sheriff. Tom brought in the books that were overdue. One was the history text—"

"You have that book handy?"

"Yes, it's on my desk."

"Mind letting me see it?"

"Of course not, but what—"

"Just let me see the book, Mary Ellen."

She got it for me. The title and subtitle were stamped in gilt on the front cover: *Sons and Daughters of the Nile. A History of Egypt from Ancient to Modern Times*. I opened it up and found the photograph that had been torn out and pasted back in, and took a good long look at it, and that was when I got my notion. The damnedest notion I'd ever had, but there it was.

I said to Mary Ellen, "I'd like to borrow this book until tomorrow."

"Check it out, you mean? But it needs to be properly repaired—"

"Just until tomorrow, Mary Ellen."

Before she could say anything else I tucked the book under my arm and went on out. I could feel the two women's eyes on my back, and I could hear them start to whisper even before I shut the door.

When I got home I sat in my Morris chair and did some studying on the history book. Then I did some studying without the book, working that notion of mine from different angles. And by golly, all the pieces fit together as pretty as you please:

WOODEN INDIAN

The missing wooden indian . . . the sawdust on Tom's shoes the morning after the theft . . . Chief Victor's illness and delirium . . . Tom and his family not letting either the tribal medicine man or Abe Fetters come along to the burial grounds . . . and the torn-out photograph in the Egyptian history book—the photograph of a sarcophagus, one of those stone coffins made in the likeness of the kings and queens and other royalty that were buried inside them.

Suppose Tom and Charlie Walks Far hadn't cut that wooden indian into pieces; suppose they'd sawed it clean in half, lengthwise, and then hollowed out both halves with hammers and wood chisels. And suppose they'd put Chief Victor's remains inside and buried Indian and indian both.

Chief Victor himself would have had to ask for it. And he might have, even if it went smack against tribal custom, if he'd been addled enough in his sickness. Could be he'd got hold of the Egyptian history book—Tom always had books lying around their shack—and could be he'd seen that photograph of the sarcophagus, and torn it out because it fascinated him, and in his delirium determined that he was royalty, too, descended from the Great Chief Victor, so why shouldn't he have a coffin like the Egyptian royalty did? Tom wouldn't have refused anything his grandfather asked, no matter how daft or heretical; he'd likely have tried to argue against it but in the end he wouldn't have refused. And since there was no time to build a sarcophagus in the old warrior's true likeness, with Chief Victory already knocking at death's door, Tom and Charlie Walks Far had had to make do with what came easy to hand.

But, hell, it was a crazy notion. Pure foolishness, even if all the pieces did fit. Must be some other explanation that made better and saner sense.

And yet . . .

Well, I *could* tell Abe Fetters about it and we *could* go out to the reservation burial ground and find out for certain. But that struck me as downright sacrilegious. Those poor Indians had enough trials and tribulations without a bunch of white men digging up their sacred burial ground. Besides which, if it did turn out to be true, then the citizens of Elk Basin would have a field day at the Indians' expense and the whole thing would get written up in newspapers around the state and maybe around the country too. And as if that wasn't bad enough, I'd have to arrest Tom and Charlie, and Henry Bandelier would sure as hell press charges against them. There'd be no justice in that. Tom couldn't go to the university and become an agronomist and help his people if he was serving a stretch in the state penitentiary.

No, I decided, the best thing for me to do was to keep that crazy notion of mine to myself. Better yet, dismiss it as a pipe dream and forget all about it.

That's just what I did. And to this day nobody in Elk Basin has ever found out what really happened to Henry Bandelier's wooden indian. Including me.

Some things, I reckon, folks are just better off not knowing.

Righteous Guns

It was hot.

And quiet—too quiet.

He walked slowly along the dusty street, one hand resting on the Colt Peacemaker pouched at his hip. The harsh midday sun made the false-fronted buildings stand out in sharp relief against a sky more white than blue, like an alkali flat turned upside down. Heat mirage shimmered beyond the livery stable in the next block, half obscuring the road that led up into the foothills west of town.

He paused opposite the Lucky Lady Saloon and Gambling Hall and stood hip-shot, listening to the silence. Nothing moved anywhere ahead of him or around him. There were no horses tied to the hitchrails, no wagons or buckboards, no townspeople making their way long the plank sidewalks. But he could feel eyes watching him from behind closed doors and shuttered windows.

Waiting, all of them—just as he was.

Waiting for the lawmen and their righteous guns.

Sweat worked its way out from under his Stetson; he wiped it away with the back of his left hand, smearing the dust-cake on his lean, sun-weathered face. His mouth tasted dry and dusty, like the street itself, and he thought of pushing in through the saloon's batwings for a beer and a shot of rye. But liquor dulled a man's thoughts, turned his reflexes slow. No liquor today.

From his shirt pocket he took out the makings and rolled a cigarette with his left hand. He scratched a sulfur match into flame on the sole of his boot. His right hand didn't move from the butt of his Peacemaker in its hand-tooled Mexican holster.

How many of them would there be? Close to a dozen, likely, maybe more. Robbing the Cattlemen's and Merchant's Bank as he'd done this morning, shooting down the bank director, Leo Furman, in cold blood when he wouldn't open the safe . . . those were about as serious crimes as there were in the Territory. There'd be plenty in the posse, all right. They'd want him bad, them and their righteous guns.

Not that it mattered much, he thought. A wry smile bent the corners of his mouth. He'd faced lawmen before, in numbers from one to twenty, in towns like this one in half a dozen states and territories throughout the West. This was nothing new. This was just more of the same for a man like him.

It was only a question of time. He'd wait, because there was nothing else for him to do. He hadn't got the money from the bank; Leo Furman had tried for a hideout gun and he'd had to shoot him before Furman could open the safe. So the only thing he could do was wait. Better to face them here, than run and have them chase him down like a dog.

When they came, he'd be ready for them.

He blew smoke into the hot still air and then commenced walking again, thinking about Leo Furman. A bossy, fussy man; like so many bank directors, he'd thought that the money other men entrusted to him gave him power over those men. Demanding, high and mighty, full of contempt—that was Furman. He wasn't sorry he'd killed the bastard. He wasn't sorry at all.

He moved on past Benson's Mercantile, the Elite Cafe, the Palace Hotel. There was still no sound, nothing stirring in the thick, milky heat. It was as if the town itself was holding its breath now.

On past the Eternal Rest Funeral Home, the blacksmith's shop, the deserted sheriff's office; heading toward the hostler's. He knew just what a menacing figure he cut, moving along that dusty, barren street: big, hard face full of angles and shadows, body leaned down to sinew and bone. Most men stood aside when he passed, avoiding his eyes. So did the women. They were afraid of him, the women; the only way he'd ever had one was by money or by force.

Sometimes, late at night, he would wake up in a strange bed or by the remains of a trailside fire and think of what might have been. An end to the vicious swath he cut through the West; an end to the shooting and the killing of decent men; righteous guns instead of his own desperate ones, or better yet, no guns at all. The love of a good woman, a small ranch on good grazing land . . .

Something moved in the alley between the blacksmith's shop and the livery.

A shadow, then a second shadow.

He tensed, alert to the sudden smell of danger. He slowed to a walk, pitched his cigarette away, let his fingers curl loosely around the butt of his Peacemaker. Squinted through the hard glare of the sunlight.

More movement inside the alley. Over on the far side of the street, too, behind Baldwin's Feed and Grain Store. Furtive sounds reached his ears: the soft sliding of boots in the dust, the faint thump of an arm or hand or leg against wood.

They were here.

Most times they came openly, riding in on their horses, weapons at the ready. Once in a while, though, they came in quiet and slinking like this, to wait in ambush in the shadows. No better than he was, then. In their own way, just as desperate.

Well, it didn't matter.

It was time, and as always, he was ready.

"*Hold it right there, Gaines!*" a voice roared suddenly from the alley. "*We've got you surrounded!*"

He bent his knees and let himself bow slightly at the middle. But he was scowling now. Gaines, the voice had said. How did they know his real name?

"*You can't get away, Gaines! Stand where you are and raise your hands over your head!*"

There was something about that voice, the odd thunderous tone of it, as if it were coming through a megaphone, that made him feel suddenly uneasy. More than uneasy—strange, dizzy. His head began to ache. The sun-baked street, the false-fronted buildings, seemed to shift in and out of focus, to take on new and different dimensions. Sunstroke, he thought. I been standing out here in the heat too long.

But it wasn't sunstroke . . .

One of the shadows in the alley shifted into view—his first clear glimpse of the law. And he stared, for the lawdog wasn't wearing Levi's or broad-brimmed hat or tin star pinned to vest or cotton shirt; wasn't carrying Winchester rifle or Colt sixgun. Strange blue uniform, blue helmet, weapon in one hand like none he'd ever seen before.

He stood blinking, confused. And saw then that the buildings didn't just have false fronts; they had false backs too, and no backs at all on some of them, just a latticework of wooden supports like sets in a play.

Sets in a *movie.*

Movie sets, TV-show sets on the back lot at Mammoth Pictures.

A dozen movies, a hundred TV shows, all starring Roy Gaines in the role of the villain . . . and Leo Furman, the director, always telling him what to do, treating him with contempt, never once letting him be good and decent, never once letting him be the hero . . . wouldn't open his safe, wouldn't give him the money he needed to pay his gambling debts, and so he'd shot Furman dead, just as he would any damned fool who crossed him . . . and then he'd come here,

RIGHTEOUS GUNS

because there was no place else for him to go, a man on the run, killer on the run, here to make still another last stand . . .

"*Gaines! You can't escape! Raise your hands over your head! Don't make us do this the hard way!*"

The hard way, the hard way, the hard way . . .

There was a jolting in his mind; the false-fronted buildings, the sun-blasted street settled back into familiar focus. Then, ahead, he could see four, five, six of the possemen fanning out toward him, keeping to cover. A grim smile formed on his mouth. He'd done all this before, so many times before. He knew just what to do. He didn't even have to think about it.

"All right," he yelled, "come and get it, boys!" His hand went down, came up again with his desperate gun blazing—

And the righteous guns cut him down.

Fergus O'Hara, Detective

ON A BALMY March afternoon in the third full year of the War Between the States, while that conflict continued to rage bloodily some two thousand miles distant, Fergus and Hattie O'Hara jostled their way along San Francisco's Embarcadero toward Long Wharf and the riverboat *Delta Star*. The half-plank, half-dirt roads and plank walks were choked with horses, mules, cargo-laden wagons—and with all manner of humanity: bearded miners and burly roustabouts and sun-darkened farmers; rope-muscled Kanakas and Filipino laborers and coolie-hatted Chinese; shrewd-eyed merchants and ruffle-shirted gamblers and bonneted ladies who might have been the wives of prominent citizens or trollops on their way to the gold fields of the Mother Lode. Both the pace and the din were furious. At exactly four P.M. some twenty steamers would leave the waterfront, bound upriver for Sacramento and Stockton and points in between.

O'Hara clung to their carpetbags and Hattie clung to O'Hara as they pushed through the throng. They could see the *Delta Star* the moment they reached Long Wharf. She was an impressive side-wheeler, one of the "floating palaces" that had adorned the Sacramento and San Joaquin rivers for more than ten years. Powered by a single-cylinder, vertical-beam engine, she was 245 feet long and had slim, graceful lines. The long rows of windows running full length both starboard and larboard along her deckhouse, where the Gentlemen's and Dining Saloons and most of the staterooms were located, refracted jewellike the rays of the afternoon sun. Above, to the stern, was the weather deck, on which stretched the "texas"; this housed luxury staterooms and cabins for the packet's officers. Some distance forward of the texas was the oblong glassed-in structure of the pilothouse.

Smiling as they approached, O'Hara said, "Now ain't she a fine lady?" He spoke with a careless brogue, the result of a strict ethnic upbringing in the Irish Channel section of New Orleans. At times this caused certain individuals to underestimate his capabilities and intelligence, which in his profession was a major asset.

"She *is* fine, Fergus," Hattie agreed. "As fine as any on the Mississippi before the war. How far did you say it was to Stockton?"

O'Hara laughed. "A hundred twenty-seven miles. One night in the lap of luxury is all we'll be having this trip, me lady."

"Pity," Hattie said. She was in her late twenties, five years younger than her husband; dark-complected, buxom. Thick black hair, worn in ringlets, was covered by a lace-decorated bonnet. She wore a gray serge traveling dress, the hem of which was now coated with dust.

O'Hara was tall and plump, and sported a luxuriant red beard of which he was inordinately proud and on which he doted every morning with scissors and comb. Like Hattie, he had mild blue eyes; unlike Hattie, and as a result of a fondness for spirits, he possessed a nose that approximated the color of his beard. He was dressed in a black frock coat, striped trousers, and a flowered vest. He carried no visible weapons, but in a holster inside his coat was a double-action revolver.

The *Delta Star's* stageplank, set aft to the main deck, was jammed with passengers and wagons; it was not twenty till four. A large group of nankeen-dressed men were congregated near the foot of the plank. All of them wore green felt shamrocks pinned to the lapels of their coats, and several were smoking thin, "long-nine" seegars. Fluttering above them on a pole held by one was a green banner with the words *Mulrooney Guards, San Francisco Company A* crudely printed on it in white.

Four of the group were struggling to lift a massive wooden crate that appeared to be quite heavy. They managed to get it aloft, grunting, and began to stagger with it to the plank. As they started up, two members of the *Delta Star's* deck crew came down and blocked their way. One of them said, "Before you go any farther, gents, show us your manifest on that box."

One of the other Mulrooneys stepped up the plank. "What manifest?" he demanded. "This ain't cargo, it's personal belongings."

"Anything heavy as that pays cargo," the deckhand said. "Rules is rules and they apply to Bluebellies same as to better folks."

"Bluebellies, is it? Ye damned Copperhead, I'll pound ye up into horsemeat!" And the Mulrooney hit the deckhand on the side of the head and knocked him down.

The second crew member stepped forward and hit the Mulrooney on the side of the head and knocked *him* down.

Another of the Guards jumped in and hit the second crewman on the side of the head and knocked *him* down.

The first deckhand got up and the first Mulrooney got up, minus his hat, and began swinging at each other. The second crewman got up and began swinging at the second Mulrooney. The other members of the Guards, shouting encouragement, formed a tight circle around the fighting men—all except for the four carrying the heavy wooden crate. Those Mulrooneys struggled up the stageplank with their burden and disappeared among the confusion on the main deck.

The fight did not last long. Several roustabouts and one of the steamer's mates hurried onto the landing and broke it up. No one seemed to have been injured, save for the two deckhands who were both unconscious. The mate seemed undecided as to what to do, finally concluded that to do nothing at all was the best recourse; he turned up the plank again. Four roustabouts carried the limp crewmen up after him, followed by the Guards who were all now loudly singing "John Brown's Body."

Hattie asked O'Hara, "Now what was *that* all about?"

"War business," he told her solemnly. "California's a long way from the battlefields, but feelings and loyalties are as strong here as in the East."

"But who are the Mulrooney Guards?"

Before O'Hara could answer, a tall man wearing a Prince Albert, who was standing next to Hattie, swung toward them and smiled and said, "I couldn't help overhearing the lady's question. If you'll pardon the intrusion, I can supply an answer."

O'Hara looked the tall man over and decided he was a gambler. He had no particular liking for gamblers, but for the most part he was tolerant of them. He said the intrusion was pardoned, introduced himself and Hattie, and learned that the tall man was John A. Colfax, of San Francisco.

Colfax had gray eyes that were both congenial and cunning. In his left hand he continually shuffled half a dozen small bronze war-issue cents—coinage that was not often seen in the West. He said, "The Mulrooney Guards is a more or less official militia company, one of several supporting the Union cause. They have two companies, one in San Francisco and one in Stockton. I imagine this one is joining the other for some sort of celebration."

"Tomorrow is St. Patrick's Day," O'Hara told him.

"Ah, yes, of course."

"Ye seem to know quite a bit about these lads, Mr. Colfax."

"I am a regular passenger on the *Delta Star*," Colfax said.

"On the Sacramento packets as well. A traveling man picks up a good deal of information."

O'Hara said blandly, "Aye, that he does."

Hattie said, "I wonder what the Mulrooneys have in that crate?"

Colfax allowed as how he had no idea. He seemed about to say something further, but the appearance of three closely grouped men, hurrying through the crowd toward the stageplank, claimed his attention. The one in the middle, O'Hara saw, wore a broadcloth suit and a nervous, harried expression; cradled in both hands against his body was a large and apparently heavy valise. The two men on either side were more roughly dressed, had revolvers holstered at their hips. Their expressions were dispassionate, their eyes watchful.

O'Hara frowned and glanced at Colfax. The gambler watched the trio climb the plank and hurry up the aft stairway; then he said quietly, as if to himself, "It appears we'll be carrying more than passengers and cargo this trip." He regarded the O'Haras again, touched his hat, said it had been a pleasure talking to them, and moved away to board the riverboat.

Hattie looked at her husband inquiringly. He said, "Gold."

"Gold, Fergus?"

"That nervous chap had the look of a banker, the other two of deputies. A bank transfer of specie or dust from here to Stockton—or so I'm thinking."

"Where will they keep it?"

"Purser's office, mayhap. Or the pilothouse."

Hattie and O'Hara climbed the plank. As they were crossing the main deck, the three men appeared again on the stairway; the one in the broadcloth suit looked considerably less nervous now. O'Hara watched them go down onto the landing. Then, shrugging, he followed Hattie up the stairs to the weather deck. They stopped at the starboard rail to await departure.

Hattie said, "What did you think of Mr. Colfax?"

"A slick-tongued lad, even for a gambler. But ye'd not want to be giving him a coin to put in a village poor box for ye."

She laughed. "He seemed rather interested in the delivery of gold, if that's what it was."

"Aye, so he did."

At exactly four o'clock the *Delta Star*'s whistle sounded; her buckets churned the water, steam poured from her twin stacks. She began to move slowly away from the wharf. All up and down the Embarcadero now, whistles sounded and the other packets commenced backing down from their landings. The waters of the bay took on a chaotic appearance as the boats maneuvered for right-of-way. Clouds of steam filled the sky; the sound of pilot whistles was angry and shrill.

Once the *Delta Star* was clear of the wharves and of other riverboats, her speed increased steadily. Hattie and O'Hara remained at the rail until San Francisco's low, sun-washed skyline had receded into the distance; then they went in search of a steward, who took them to their stateroom. Its windows faced larboard, but its entrance was located inside a tunnellike hallway down the center of the texas. Spacious and opulent, the cabin contained carved rosewood paneling and red plush upholstery. Hattie said she thought it was grand. O'Hara, who had never been particularly impressed by Victorian elegance, said he imagined she would be wanting to freshen up a bit—and that, so as not to be disturbing her, he would take a stroll about the decks.

"Stay away from the liquor buffet," Hattie said. "The day is young, if I make my meaning clear."

O'Hara sighed. "I had no intention of visiting the liquor buffet," he lied, and sighed again, and left the stateroom.

He wandered aft, past the officers' quarters. When he

emerged from the texas he found himself confronted by the huge A-shaped gallows frame that housed the cylinder, valve gear, beam and crank of the walking-beam engine. Each stroke of the piston produced a mighty roar and hiss of escaping steam. The noise turned O'Hara around and sent him back through the texas to the forward stairway.

Ahead of him as he started down were two men who had come out of the pilothouse. One was tall, with bushy black hair and a thick mustache—apparently a passenger. The second wore a square-billed cap and the sort of stern, authoritative look that would have identified him as the *Delta Star*'s pilot even without the cap. At this untroubled point in the journey, the packet would be in the hands of a cub apprentice.

The door to the Gentlemen's Saloon kept intruding on O'Hara's thoughts as he walked about the deckhouse. Finally he went down to the main deck. Here, in the open areas and in the shedlike expanse beneath the superstructures, deck passengers and cargo were pressed together in noisy confusion: men and women and children, wagons and animals and chickens in coops; sacks, bales, boxes, hogsheads, cords of bull pine for the roaring fireboxes under the boilers. And, too, the Mulrooney Guards, who were loosely grouped near the taffrail, alternately singing "The Girl I Left Behind Me" and passing around jugs of what was likely poteen—a powerful homemade Irish whiskey.

O'Hara sauntered near the group, stood with his back against a stanchion, and began to shave cuttings from his tobacco plug into his briar. One of the Mulrooneys—small and fair and feisty looking—noticed him, studied his luxuriant red beard, and then approached him carrying one of the jugs. Without preamble he demanded to know if the gentleman were Irish. O'Hara said he was, with great dignity. The Mulrooney slapped him on the back. "I knew it!" he said effusively. "Me name's Billy Culligan. Have a drap of the crayture."

O'Hara decided Hattie had told him only to stay away from the buffet. There was no deceit in accepting hospitality from fellows of the Auld Sod. He took the jug, drank deeply, and allowed as how it was a fine crayture, indeed. Then he introduced himself, saying that he and the missus were traveling to Stockton on a business matter.

"Ye won't be conducting business on the morrow, will ye?"

"On St. Pat's Day?" O'Hara was properly shocked.

"Boyo, I like ye," Culligan said. "How would ye like to join in on the biggest St. Pat's Day celebration in the entire sovereign state of California?"

"I'd like nothing better."

"Then come to Green Park, on the north of Stockton, 'twixt nine and ten and tell the lads ye're a friend of Billy Culligan. There'll be a parade, and all the food and liquor ye can hold. Oh, it'll be a fine celebration, lad!"

O'Hara said he and the missus would be there, meaning it. Culligan offered another drink of poteen, which O'Hara casually accepted. Then the little Mulrooney stepped forward and said in a conspiratorial voice, "Come round here to the taffrail just before we steam into Stockton on the morrow. We've a plan to start off St. Pat's Day with a mighty salute—part of the reason we sent our wives and wee ones ahead on the *San Joaquin*. Ye won't want to be missing that either." Before O'Hara could ask him what he meant by "mighty salute," he and his jug were gone into the midst of the other Guards.

"Me lady," O'Hara said contentedly, "that was a meal fit for royalty and no doubt about it."

Hattie agreed that it had been a sumptuous repast as they walked from the Dining Saloon to the texas stairway. The evening was mild, with little breeze and no sign of the thick tule fog that often made Northern California riverboating a hazardous proposition. The *Delta Star*—aglow with hundreds of lights—had come through the Carquinez Straits, passed Chipp's Island, and was now entering the San Joaquin River. A pale moon silvered the water, turned a ghostly white the long stretches of fields along both banks.

On the weather deck, they stood close together at the larboard rail, not far from the pilothouse. For a couple of minutes they were alone. Then footsteps sounded and O'Hara turned to see the ship's captain and pilot returning from their dinner. Touching his cap, the captain—a lean, graying man of fifty-odd—wished them good evening. The pilot merely grunted.

The O'Haras continued to stand looking out at the willows and cottonwoods along the riverbank. Then, suddenly, an explosive, angry cry came from the pilothouse, startling them both. This was followed by muffled voices, another sharp exclamation, movement not clearly perceived through the window glass and beyond partially drawn rear curtains, and several sharp blasts on the pilot whistle.

Natural curiosity drew O'Hara away from the rail, hurrying; Hattie was close behind him. The door to the pilothouse stood open when they reached it, and O'Hara turned inside by one step. The enclosure was almost as opulent as their stateroom, but he noticed its appointments only peripherally. What captured his full attention was three men now grouped before the wheel, and the four items on the floor close to and against the starboard bulkhead.

The pilot stood clutching two of the wheel spokes, red-faced with anger; the captain was bending over the kneeling figure of the third man—a young blond individual wearing a buttoned-up sack coat and baggy trousers, both of which were streaked with dust and soot and grease. The blond lad was making soft moaning sounds, holding the back of his head cupped in one palm.

One of the items on the floor was a steel pry bar. The others were a small safe bolted to the bulkhead, a black valise—the one O'Hara had seen carried by the nervous man and his two bodyguards—and a medium-sized iron strongbox, just large enough to have fit inside the valise. The safe door, minus its combination dial, stood wide open; the valise and a strongbox were also open. All three were quite obviously empty.

The pilot jerked the bell knobs, signaling an urgent request to the engineer for a lessening of speed, and began barking stand-by orders into a speaking tube. His was the voice which had startled Hattie and O'Hara. The captain was saying to the blond man, "It's a miracle we didn't drift out of the channel and run afoul of a snag—a miracle, Chadwick."

"I can't be held to blame, sir," Chadwick said defensively. "Whoever it was hit me from behind. I was sitting at the wheel when I heard the door open and thought it was you and Mr. Bridgeman returning from supper, so I didn't even bother to turn. The next thing, my head seemed to explode. That is all I know."

He managed to regain his feet and moved stiffly to a red plush sofa, hitching up his trousers with one hand; the other still held the back of his head. Bridgeman, the pilot, banged down the speaking tube, then spun the wheel a half-turn to larboard. As he did the last, he glanced over his shoulder and saw O'Hara and Hattie. "Get out of here!" he shouted at them. "There is nothing here for you."

"Perhaps, now, that isn't true," O'Hara said mildly. "Ye've had a robbery, have ye not?"

"That is none of your affair."

Boldly O'Hara came deeper into the pilothouse, motioning Hattie to close the door. She did so. Bridgeman yelled, "I told you to get out of here! Who do you think you are?"

"Fergus O'Hara—operative of the Pinkerton Police Agency."

Bridgeman stared at him, open-mouthed. The captain and Chadwick had shifted their attention to him as well. At length, in a less harsh tone, the pilot said, "Pinkerton Agency?"

"Of Chicago, Illinois; Allan Pinkerton, Principal."

O'Hara produced his billfold, extracted from it the letter from Allan Pinkerton and the Chicago & Eastern Central Railroad Pass, both of which identified him, as the bearer of these documents, to be a Pinkerton Police agent. He showed them to both Bridgeman and the captain.

"What would a Pinkerton man be doing way out here in California?" the captain asked.

"Me wife Hattie and me are on the trail of a gang that has been terrorizing Adams Express coaches. We've traced them to San Francisco and now have reliable information they're to be found in Stockton."

"Your *wife* is a Pinkerton agent too? A *woman* . . . ?"

O'Hara looked at him as if he might be a dullard. "Ye've never heard of Miss Kate Warne, one of the agency's most trusted Chicago operatives? No, I don't suppose ye have. Well, me wife has no official capacity, but since one of the leaders of this gang is reputed to be a woman, and since Hattie has assisted me in the past, women being able to obtain information in places men cannot, I've brought her along."

Bridgeman said from the wheel, "Well, we can use a trained detective after what has happened here."

O'Hara nodded. "Is it gold ye've had stolen?"

"Gold—yes. How did you know that?"

He told them of witnessing the delivery of the valise at Long Wharf. He asked then, "How large an amount is involved?"

"Forty thousand dollars," the captain said.

O'Hara whistled. "That's a fair considerable sum."

"To put it mildly, sir."

"Was it specie or dust?"

"Dust. An urgent consignment from the California Merchant's Bank to their branch in Stockton."

"How many men had foreknowledge of the shipment?"

"The officials of the bank, Mr. Bridgeman, and myself."

"No other officers of the packet?"

"No."

"Would you be telling me, Captain, who was present when the delivery was made this afternoon?"

"Mr. Bridgeman and I, and a friend of his visiting in San Francisco—a newspaperman from Nevada."

O'Hara remembered the tall man with bushy hair who had been with the pilot earlier. "Can ye vouch for this newspaperman?" he asked Bridgeman.

"I can. His reputation is unimpeachable."

"Has anyone other than he been here since the gold was brought aboard?"

"Not to my knowledge."

Chadwick said that no one had come by while he was on duty; and none of them had noticed anyone shirking about at any time. The captain said sourly, "It appears as though almost any man on this packet could be the culprit. Just how do you propose we find out which one, Mr. O'Hara?"

O'Hara did not reply. He bent to examine the safe. The combination dial appeared to have been snapped off, by a hand with experience at such villainous business. The valise and the strong-box had also been forced. The pry bar was an ordinary tool and had likely also been used as a weapon to knock Chadwick unconscious.

He straightened and moved about the enclosure, studying each fixture. Then he got down on hands and knees and peered under both the sofa and a blackened winter stove. It was under the stove that he found the coin.

His fingers grasped it, closed it into his palm. Standing again, he glanced at the coin and saw that it was made of bronze, a small war-issue cent piece shinily new and free of dust or soot. A smile plucked at the edges of his mouth as he slipped the coin into his vest pocket.

Bridgeman said, "Did you find something?"

"Perhaps. Then again, perhaps not."

O'Hara came forward, paused near where Bridgeman stood at the wheel. Through the windshield he could see the moonlit waters of the San Joaquin. He could also see, as a result of the pilothouse lamps and the darkness without, his own dim reflection in the glass. He thought his stern expression was rather like the one Allan Pinkerton himself possessed.

Bridgeman suggested that crewmen be posted on the lower decks throughout the night, as a precaution in the event the culprit had a confederate with a boat somewhere along the route and intended to leave the packet in the wee hours. The captain thought this was a good idea; so did O'Hara.

He was ready to leave, but the captain had a few more words for him. "I am grateful for your professional assistance, Mr. O'Hara, but as master of the *Delta Star* the primary investigative responsibility is mine. Please inform me immediately if you learn anything of significance."

O'Hara said he would.

"Also, I intend my inquiries to be discreet, so as not to alarm the passengers. I'll expect yours to be the same."

"Discretion is me middle name," O'Hara assured him.

A few moments later, he and Hattie were on their way back along the larboard rail to the texas. Hattie, who had been silent during their time in the pilothouse, started to speak, but O'Hara overrode her. "I know what ye're going to say, me lady, and it'll do no good. Me mind's made up. The opportunity to sniff out forty thousand in missing gold is one I'll not pass up."

He left Hattie at the door to their stateroom and hurried to the deckhouse, where he entered the Gentlemen's Saloon. It was a long room, with a liquor buffet at one end and private tables and card layouts spread throughout. A pall of tobacco smoke as thick as tule fog hung in the crowded enclosure.

O'Hara located the shrewd, handsome features of John A. Colfax at a table aft. Two other men were with him: a portly individual with sideburns like miniature tumbleweeds, and the mustached Nevada reporter. They were playing draw poker. O'Hara was not surprised to see that most of the stakes—gold specie and greenbacks—were in front of Colfax.

Casually, O'Hara approached the table and stopped behind an empty chair next to the portly man, just as Colfax claimed a pot with four treys. He said, "Good evening, gentlemen."

Colfax greeted him unctuously, asked if he were enjoying the voyage thus far. O'Hara said he was, and observed that the gambler seemed to be enjoying it too, judging from the stack of legal tender before him. Colfax just smiled. But the portly man said in grumbling tones, "I should damned well say so. He has been taking my money for three solid hours."

"Aye? That long?"

"Since just after dinner."

"Ye've been playing without pause since then?"

"Nearly so," the newspaperman said. Through the tendrils of smoke from his cigar, he studied O'Hara with mild blue eyes. "Why do you ask, sir?"

"Oh, I was thinking I saw Mr. Colfax up on the weather deck about an hour ago. Near the pilothouse."

"You must have mistaken someone else for me," Colfax said. Now that the draw game had been momentarily suspended, he had produced a handful of war-issue coins and begun to toy with them as he had done at Long Wharf. "I did leave the table for a few minutes about an hour ago, but only to use the lavatory. I haven't been on the weather deck at all this trip."

O'Hara saw no advantage in pressing the matter. He pretended to notice for the first time the one-cent pieces Colfax was shuffling. "Lucky coins, Mr. Colfax?"

"These? Why, yes. I won a sackful of them on a wager once and my luck has been good ever since." Disarming smile. "Gamblers are superstitious about such things, you know."

"Ye don't see many coins like that in California."

"True. They are practically worthless out here."

"So worthless," the reporter said, "that I have seen them used to decorate various leather goods."

The portly man said irritably, "To hell with lucky coins and such nonsense. Are we going to play poker or have a gabfest?"

"Poker, by all means," Colfax said. He slipped the war-issue cents into a pocket of his Prince Albert and reached for the cards. His interest in O'Hara seemed to have vanished.

The reporter, however, was still looking at him with curiosity. "Perhaps you'd care to join us?"

O'Hara declined, saying he had never had any luck with the pasteboards. Then he left the saloon and went in search of the *Delta Star*'s purser. It took him ten minutes to find the man, and thirty seconds to learn that John A. Colfax did not have a stateroom either in the texas or on the deckhouse. The purser, who knew Colfax as a regular passenger, said wryly that the gambler would spend the entire voyage in the Gentlemen's Saloon, having gullible citizens for a ride.

O'Hara returned to the saloon, this time to avail himself of the liquor buffet. He ordered a shot of rye from a bartender who owned a resplendent handlebar moustache, and tossed it down without his customary enjoyment. Immediately he ordered another.

Colfax might well be his man; there was the war-issue coin he'd found under the pilothouse stove, and the fact that Colfax had left the poker game at about the time of the robbery. And yet . . . what could he have done with the gold? The weight of forty thousand in dust was considerable; he could not very well carry it in his pockets. He had been gone from the poker game long enough to commit the robbery, perhaps, but hardly long enough to have also hidden the spoils.

There were other factors weighing against Colfax, too. One: gentlemen gamblers made considerable sums of money at their trade; they seldom found it necessary to resort to baser thievery. Two: how could Colfax, while sitting here in the saloon, have known when only one man would be present in the pilothouse? An accomplice might have been on watch—but if there were such a second party, why hadn't *he* committed the robbery himself?

O'Hara scowled, put away his second rye. If Colfax wasn't the culprit, then who was? And what was the significance of the coin he had found in the pilothouse?

Perhaps the coin had no significance at all; but his instincts told him it did, and he had always trusted his instincts. If not to Colfax, then to whom did it point? Answer: to no one, and to everyone. Even though war-issue cents were uncommon in California, at least half a dozen men presently on board might have one or two in their pockets.

A remark passed by the newspaperman came back to him: such coins were used to decorate various leather goods. Aye, that was a possibility. If the guilty man had been wearing a holster or vest or some other article adorned with the cent pieces, one might have popped loose unnoticed.

O'Hara slid the coin from his pocket and examined it carefully. There were small scratches on its surface that might have been made by stud fasteners, but he couldn't be sure. The scratches might also have been caused by any one of a hundred other means—and the coin could still belong to John A. Colfax.

Returning it to his vest pocket, O'Hara considered the idea of conducting a search for a man wearing leather ornamented with bronze war coins. And dismissed it immediately as folly. He could roam the *Delta Star* all night and not encounter even two-thirds of the passengers. Or he might find someone wearing such an article who would turn out to be completely innocent. And what if the robber had discovered the loss of the coin and chucked the article overboard?

Frustration began to assail him now. But it did not dull his determination. If any man aboard the *Delta Star* could fetch up both the thief and the gold before the packet reached Stockton, that man was Fergus O'Hara; and by damn, if such were humanly possible, he meant to do it!

He left the saloon again and went up to the pilothouse. Bridgeman was alone at the wheel. "What news, O'Hara?" he asked.

"None as yet. Would ye know where the captain is?"

Bridgeman shook his head. "Young fool Chadwick was feeling dizzy from that blow on the head; the captain took him to his quarters just after you and your wife left, and then went to make his inquiries. I expect he's still making 'em."

O'Hara sat on the red plush sofa, packed and lighted his pipe, and let his mind drift along various channels. After a time something in his memory flickered like a guttering candle—and then died before he could steady the flame. When he was unable to rekindle the flame he roared forth with a venomous ten-jointed oath that startled even Bridgeman.

Presently the captain returned to the pilothouse. He and O'Hara exchanged identical expectant looks, which immediately told each that the other had uncovered nothing of significance. Verbal confirmation of this was brief, after which the captain said bleakly, "The prospects are grim, Mr. O'Hara. Grim, indeed."

"We've not yet come into Stockton," O'Hara reminded him.

The captain sighed. "We have no idea of who is guilty, thus no idea of where to find the gold . . . if in fact it is still on board. We haven't the manpower for a search of packet and passengers before our arrival. And afterward—I don't see how we can hope to hold everyone on board while the authorities are summoned and a search mounted. Miners are a hotheaded lot; so are those Irish militiamen. We would likely have a riot on our hands."

O'Hara had nothing more to say. By all the saints, *he* was not yet ready to admit defeat. He bid the captain and Bridgeman good night, and spent the next hour prowling the decks and cudgeling his brain. It seemed to him that he had seen and heard enough since the robbery to *know* who it was he was after and where the missing gold could be found. If only he could bring forth one scrap of this knowledge from his memory, he was certain the others would follow . . .

Maddeningly, however, no scrap was forthcoming. Not while he prowled the decks, not after he returned to his stateroom (Hattie, he was relieved to find, was already fast asleep)—and not when the first light of dawn crept into the sky beyond the window.

When the *Delta Star* came out of one of the snakelike bends in the river and started down the last long reach to Stockton, O'Hara was standing with Hattie at the starboard deckhouse rail. It was just past seven-thirty—a spring-crisp, cloudless St. Patrick's Day morning—and the steamer would dock in another thirty minutes.

O'Hara was in a foul humor: three-quarters frustration and one-quarter lack of sleep. He had left the stateroom at six o'clock and gone up to the pilothouse and found the captain, Bridgeman, and Chadwick drinking coffee thickened with molasses. They had nothing to tell him. And their humors had been no better than his; it seemed that as a result of O'Hara's failure to perform as advertised, he had fallen out of favor with them.

Staring down at the slow-moving waters frothed by the sidewheel, he told himself for the thousandth time: Ye've got the answer, ye know ye do. Think, lad! Dredge it up before it's too late . . .

A voice beside him said, "Fine morning, isn't it?"

Irritably O'Hara turned his head and found himself looking

into the cheerfully smiling visage of the Nevada newspaperman. The bushy-haired lad's eyes were red-veined from a long night in the Gentlemen's Saloon, but this did not seem to have had any effect on his disposition.

O'Hara grunted. "Is it?" he said grumpily. "Ye sound as if ye have cause for rejoicing. Did ye win a hatful of specie from the gambler Colfax last night?"

"Unfortunately, no. I lost a fair sum, as a matter of fact. Gambling is one of my sadder vices, along with a fondness for the social drink. But then, a man may have no bad habits and have worse."

O'Hara grunted again and looked out over the broad, yellowish land of the San Joaquin Valley.

The reporter's gaze was on the river. "Clear as a mirror, isn't it?" he said nostalgically. "Not at all like the Mississippi. I remember when I was a boy . . ."

O'Hara had jerked upright, into a posture as rigid as an obelisk. He stood that way for several seconds. Then he said explosively, "In the name of Patrick and all the saints!"

Hattie said with alarm in her voice, "Fergus, what is it?"

O'Hara grinned at her, swung around to the newspaperman and clapped him exuberantly on the shoulder. "Lad, it may yet be a fine a morning. It may yet be, indeed."

He told Hattie to wait there for him, left her and the bewildered reporter at the rail, and hurried down to the aft stairway. On the weather deck, he moved aft of the texas and stopped before the gallows frame.

There was no one in the immediate vicinity. O'Hara stepped up close to the frame and eased his head and both arms inside the vent opening, avoiding the machinery of the massive walking-beam. Heat and the heavy odor of cylinder oil assailed him; the throb of the piston was almost deafening.

With his left hand he felt along the interior wall of the frame, his fingertips encountering a greasy build-up of oil and dust. It was only a few seconds before they located a metal hook screwed into the wood. A new hook, free of grease; he was able to determine that by touching it with the clean fingers of his right hand. Nothing was suspended from the hook, but O'Hara was now certain that something had been during most of the night.

He was also certain that he knew where it could be found at this very moment.

When he withdrew his head and arms from the vent opening, grease stained his hands and his coat and shirt sleeves, and he was sweating from the heat. He used his handkerchief, then hastened across to enter the texas. There were identifying plates screwed to the doors of the officers' cabins; he stopped before the one he wanted, drew his coat away from his revolver and laid the fingers of his right hand on its grip. With his left hand he rapped on the door panel.

There was no response.

He knocked again, waited, then took out his pocket knife. The door latch yielded in short order to rapid manipulations with one of the blades. He slipped inside and shut the door behind him.

A brief look around convinced him that the most likely hiding place was a dark corner formed by the single bunkbed and an open-topped wooden tool carrier. And that in fact was where he found what he was looking for: a wide leather belt ornamented with bronze war-issue coins, and a greasy calfskin grip. He drew the bag out, worked at the locked catch with his knife, and got it open.

The missing gold was inside, in two-score small pouches.

O'Hara looked at the sacks for several seconds, smiling. Then he found himself thinking of the captain, and of the bank in Stockton that urgently awaited the consignment. He sobered, shook himself mentally. This was neither the time nor the place for rumination; there was still much to be done. He refastened the grip, hefted it, and started to rise.

Scraping noise on the deck outside. Then the cabin door burst open, and the man whose quarters these were, the man who had stolen the gold, stood framed in the opening.

Chadwick, the cub pilot.

Recognition darkened his face with the blood of rage. He growled, "So you found out, did you? You damned Pinkerton meddler!" And he launched himself across the cabin.

O'Hara moved to draw his revolver too late. By then Chadwick was on him. The young pilot's shoulder struck the carpetbag that O'Hara thrust up defensively, sandwiched it between them as they went crashing into the larboard bulkhead. The impact broke them apart. O'Hara spilled sideways across the bunk, with the grip between his legs, and cracked his head on the rounded projection of wood that served as headboard. An eruption of pain blurred his vision, kept him from reacting as quickly as he might have. Chadwick was on him again before he could disengage himself from the bag.

A wild blow grazed the side of O'Hara's head. He threw up a forearm, succeeded in warding off a second blow but not a third. That one connected solidly with his jaw, and his vision went cockeyed again.

He was still conscious, but he seemed to have momentarily lost all power of movement. The flailing weight that was Chadwick lifted from him. There were scuffling sounds, then the sharp running slap of boots receding across the cabin and on the deck outside.

O'Hara's jaw and the back of his head began a simultaneous and painful throbbing; at the same time strength seemed to flow back into his arms and legs. Shaking his head to clear his vision, he swung off the bunk and let loose with a many-jointed oath that even his grandfather, who had always sworn he could out-cuss Old Nick himself, would have been proud to call his own. When he could see again he realized that Chadwick had caught up the calfskin grip and taken it with him. He hobbled to the door and turned to larboard out of it, the way the running steps had gone.

Chadwick, hampered by the weight and bulk of the grip, was at the bottom of the aft stairway when O'Hara reached the top. He glanced upward, saw O'Hara, and began to race frantically toward the nearby main-deck staircase. He banged into passengers, scattering them; whirled a fat woman around like a ballerina executing a pirouette and sent the reticule she had been carrying over the rail into the river.

Men commenced calling in angry voices and milling about as O'Hara tumbled down the stairs to the deckhouse. A bearded, red-shirted miner stepped into Chadwick's path at the top of the main-deck stairway; without slowing, the cub pilot bowled him over as if he were a giant ninepin and went down the stairs in a headlong dash. O'Hara lurched through the confusion of passengers and descended after him, cursing eloquently all the while.

Chadwick shoved two startled Chinese out of the way at the foot of the stairs and raced toward the taffrail, looking back over his shoulder. The bloody fool was going to jump into the river, O'Hara thought. And when he did, the weight of the gold would take both him and the bag straight to the bottom—

All at once O'Hara became aware that there were not many passengers inhabiting the aft section of the main deck, when there should have been a clotted mass of them. Some of those who were present had heard the commotion on the upper deck and been drawn to the staircase; the rest were split into two groups, one lining the larboard rail and the other lining the starboard, and their attention was held by a different spectacle. Some were murmuring excitedly; others looked amused;

still others wore apprehensive expressions. The center section of the deck opposite the taffrail was completely cleared.

The reason for this was that a small, rusted, and very old half-pounder had been set up on wooden chocks at the taffrail, aimed downriver like an impolitely pointing finger.

Beside the cannon was a keg of black powder and a charred-looking ramrod.

And surrounding the cannon were the Mulrooney Guards, one of whom held a firebrand poised above the fuse vent and all of whom were now loudly singing "The Wearing of the Green."

O'Hara knew in that moment what it was the Mulrooneys had had secreted inside their wooden crate, and why they had been so anxious to get it aboard without having the contents examined; and he knew the meaning of Billy Culligan's remark about planning to start off St. Patrick's day with a mighty salute. He stopped running and opened his mouth to shout at Chadwick, who was still fleeing and still looking back over his shoulder. He could not recall afterward if he actually *did* shout or not; if so, it was akin to whispering in a thunderstorm.

The Mulrooney cannoneer touched off the fuse. The other Mulrooney Guards scattered, still singing. The watching passengers huddled farther back, some averting their eyes. Chadwick kept on running toward the taffrail.

And the cannon, as well as the keg of black powder, promptly blew up.

The *Delta Star* lurched and rolled with the sudden concussion. A great sweeping cloud of sulfurous black smoke enveloped the riverboat. O'Hara caught hold of one of the uprights in the starboard rail and clung to it, coughing and choking. Too much black powder and not enough bracing, he thought. Then he thought: I hope Hattie had the good sense to stay where she was on the deckhouse.

The steamer was in a state of bedlam: everyone on each of the three decks screaming or shouting. Some of the passengers thought a boiler had exploded, a common steamboat hazard. When the smoke finally began to dissipate, O'Hara looked in the direction of the center taffrail and discovered that most of it, like the cannon, was missing. The deck in that area was blackened and scarred, some of the boarding torn into splinters.

But there did not seem to have been any casualties. A few passengers had received minor injuries, most of them Mulrooney Guards, and several were speckled with black soot. No one had fallen overboard. Even Chadwick had miraculously managed to survive the concussion, despite his proximity to the cannon when it and the powder keg had gone up. He was moaning feebly and moving his arms and legs, looking like a bedraggled chimney sweep, when O'Hara reached his side.

The grip containing the gold had fared somewhat better. Chadwick had been shielding it with his body at the moment of the blast, and while it was torn open and the leather pouches scattered about, most of the sacks were intact. One or two had split open, and particles of gold dust glittered in the sooty air. The preponderance of passengers were too concerned with their own welfare to notice; those who did stared with disbelief but kept their distance, for no sooner had O'Hara reached Chadwick than the captain and half a dozen of the deck crew arrived.

"Chadwick?" the captain said in amazement. *"Chadwick's the thief?"*

"Aye, he's the one."

"But . . . what happened? What was he doing here with the gold?"

"I was chasing him, the spalpeen."

"You were? Then . . . you knew of his guilt before the explosion? How?"

"I'll explain it all to ye later," O'Hara said. "Right now there's me wife to consider."

He left the bewildered captain and his crew to attend to Chadwick and the gold, and went to find Hattie.

Shortly past nine, an hour after the *Delta Star* had docked at the foot of Stockton's Center Street, O'Hara stood with Hattie and a group of men on the landing. He wore his last clean suit, a broadcloth, and a bright green tie in honor of St. Patrick's Day. The others, clustered around him, were Bridgeman, the captain, the Nevada reporter, a hawkish man who was Stockton's sheriff, and two officials of the California Merchants Bank. Chadwick had been removed to the local jail in the company of a pair of deputies and a doctor. The Mulrooney Guards, after medical treatment, a severe reprimand, and a promise to pay all damages to the packet, had been released to continue their merrymaking in Green Park.

The captain was saying, "We are all deeply indebted to you, Mr. O'Hara. It would have been a black day if Chadwick had succeeded in escaping with the gold—a black day for us all."

"I only did me duty," O'Hara said solemnly.

"It is unfortunate that the California Merchants Bank cannot offer you a reward," one of the bank officials said. "However, we are not a wealthy concern, as our urgent need for the consignment of dust attests. But I don't suppose you could accept a reward in any case; the Pinkertons never do, I'm told."

"Aye, that's true."

Bridgeman said, "Will you explain now how you knew Chadwick was the culprit? And how he accomplished the theft? He refused to confess, you know."

O'Hara nodded. He told them of finding the war-issue coin under the pilothouse stove; his early suspicions of the gambler, Colfax; the reporter's remark that such coins were being used in California to decorate leather goods; his growing certainty that he had seen and heard enough to piece together the truth, and yet his maddening inability to cudgel forth the necessary scraps from his memory.

"It wasn't until this morning that the doors in me mind finally opened," he said. He looked at the newspaperman. "It was this gentleman that gave me the key."

The reporter was surprised. "*I* gave you the key?"

"Ye did," O'Hara told him. "Ye said of the river: *Clear as a mirror, isn't it?* Do ye remember saying that, while we were together at the rail?"

"I do. But I don't see—"

"It was the word *mirror*," O'Hara said. "It caused me to think of reflection, and all at once I was recalling how I'd been able to see me own image in the pilothouse windshield soon after the robbery. Yet Chadwick claimed he was sitting in the pilot's seat when he heard the door open just before he was struck, and that he didn't turn because he thought it was the captain and Mr. Bridgeman returning from supper. But if I was able to see *me* reflection in the glass, Chadwick would sure have been able to see his—and anybody creeping up behind him.

"Then I recalled something else: Chadwick had his coat buttoned when I first entered the pilothouse, on a warm night like the last. Why? And why did his trousers look so baggy, as though they might fall down?

"Well, then, the answer was this: After Chadwick broke open the safe and the strongbox, his problem was what to do with the gold. He couldn't risk a trip to his quarters while he was alone in the pilothouse; he might be seen, and there was also the possibility that the *Delta Star* would run into a bar or snag if she slipped off course. D'ye recall saying it was a miracle such hadn't happened, Captain, thinking as ye were then that Chadwick had been unconscious for some time?"

The captain said he did.

"So Chadwick had to have the gold on his person," O'Hara said, "when you and Mr. Bridgeman found him, and when Hattie and I entered soon afterward. He couldn't have removed it until later, when he claimed to be feeling dizzy and you escorted him to his cabin. That, now, is the significance of the buttoned coat and the baggy trousers.

"What he must have done was to take off his belt, the wide one decorated with war-issue coins that I found in his cabin, and use it to strap the gold pouches above his waist—a makeshift money belt, ye see. He was in such a rush, for fear of being found out, that he failed to notice when one of the coins popped loose and rolled under the stove.

"Once he had the pouches secured, he waited until he heard Mr. Bridgeman and the captain returning, the while tending to his piloting duties; then he lay down on the floor and pretended to've been knocked senseless. He kept his loose coat buttoned for fear someone would notice the thickness about his upper middle, and that he was no longer wearing his belt in its proper place; and he kept hitching up his trousers because he wasn't wearing the belt in its proper place."

Hattie took her husband's arm. "Fergus, what did Chadwick do with the gold afterward? Did he have it hidden in his quarters all along?"

"No, me lady. I expect he was afraid of a search, so first chance he had he put the gold into the calfskin grip and then hung the grip from a metal hook inside the gallows frame."

The Stockton sheriff asked, "How could you possibly have deduced that fact?"

"While in the pilothouse after the robbery," O'Hara said, "I noticed that Chadwick's coat was soiled with dust and soot from his lying on the floor. But it also showed streaks of grease, which couldn't have come from the floor. When the other pieces fell into place this morning, I reasoned that he might have picked up the grease marks while making preparations to hide the gold. My consideration then was that he'd have wanted a place close to his quarters, and the only such place with grease about it was the gallows frame. The hook I discovered inside was new and free of grease; Chadwick, therefore, must have put it there only recently—tonight, in fact, thus accounting for the grease on his coat."

"Amazing detective work," the reporter said, "simply amazing."

Everyone else agreed.

"You really are a fine detective, Fergus O'Hara," Hattie said. "Amazing, indeed."

O'Hara said nothing. Now that they were five minutes parted from the others, walking alone together along Stockton's dusty main street, he had begun scowling and grumbling to himself.

Hattie ventured, "It's a splendid, sunny St. Patrick's Day. Shall we join the festivities in Green Park?"

"We've nothing to celebrate," O'Hara muttered.

"Still thinking about the gold, are you?"

"And what else would I be thinking about?" he said. "Fine detective—faugh! Some consolation *that* is!"

It was Hattie's turn to be silent.

O'Hara wondered sourly what those lads back at the landing would say if they knew the truth of the matter: That he was no more a Pinkerton operative than were the Mulrooney Guards. That he had only been *impersonating* one toward his own ends, in this case and others since he had taken the railroad pass and letter of introduction off the chap in Saint Louis the previous year—the Pinkerton chap who'd foolishly believed he was taking O'Hara to jail. That he had wanted the missing pouches of gold for himself and Hattie. And that he, Fergus

O'Hara, was the finest *confidence man* in these sovereign United States, come to Stockton, California, to have for a ride a banker who intended to cheat the government by buying up Indian land.

Well, those lads would never know any of this, because he had duped them all—brilliantly, as always. And for nothing. Nothing!

He moaned aloud, "Forty thousand in gold, Hattie. Forty thousand that I was holding in me hands, clutched fair to me black heart, when that rascal Chadwick burst in on me. Two more minutes, just two more minutes . . ."

"It was Providence," she said. "You were never meant to have that gold, Fergus."

"What d'ye mean? The field was white for the sickle—"

"Not a bit of that," Hattie said. "And if you'll be truthful with yourself, you'll admit you enjoyed every minute of your play-acting of a detective; every minute of the explaining just now of your brilliant deductions."

"I didn't," O'Hara lied weakly. "I hate detectives . . ."

"Bosh. I'm glad the gold went to its rightful owners, and you should be too because your heart is about as black as this sunny morning. You've only stolen from dishonest men in all the time I've known you. Why, if you *had* succeeded in filching the gold, you'd have begun despising yourself sooner than you realize—not only because it belongs to honest citizens but because you would have committed the crime on St. Patrick's Day. If you stop to consider it, you wouldn't commit *any* crime on St. Pat's Day, now would you?"

O'Hara grumbled and glowered, but he was remembering his thoughts in Chadwick's cabin, when he had held the gold in his hands—thoughts of the captain's reputation and possible loss of position, and of the urgent need of the new branch bank in Stockton. He was not at all sure, now, that he would have kept the pouches if Chadwick had not burst in on him. He might well have returned them to the captain. Confound it, that was just what he would have done.

Hattie was right about St. Pat's Day, too. He would not feel decent if he committed a crime on—

Abruptly, he stopped walking. Then he put down their luggage and said, "You wait here, me lady. There's something that needs doing before we set off for Green Park."

Before Hattie could speak, he was on his way through clattering wagons and carriages to where a towheaded boy was scuffling with a mongrel dog. He halted before the boy. "Now then, lad, how would ye like to have a dollar for twenty minutes good work?"

The boy's eyes grew wide. "What do I have to do, mister?"

O'Hara removed from the inside pocket of his coat an expensive gold American Horologe watch, which happened to be in his possession as the result of a momentary lapse in good sense and fingers made nimble during his misspent youth in New Orleans. He extended it to the boy.

"Take this down to the *Delta Star* steamboat and look about for a tall gentleman with a mustache and a fine head of bushy hair, a newspaperman from Nevada. When ye've found him, give him the watch and tell him Mr. Fergus O'Hara came upon it, is returning it, and wishes him a happy St. Patrick's Day."

"What's his name, mister?" the boy asked. "It'll help me find him quicker."

O'Hara could not seem to recall it, if he had ever heard it in the first place. He took the watch again, opened the hunting-style case, and saw that a name had been etched in flowing script on the dustcover. He handed the watch back to the boy.

"Clemens, it is," O'Hara said then. "A Mr. Samuel Langhorne Clemens . . ."

All the Long Years

I CAUGHT HIM some past noon on the second day, over on the west edge of my range near Little Creek.

Thing was, he wasn't much of a cow thief. He'd come onto my land in broad daylight, bold as brass, instead of nightherding and then doing his brand-burning elsewhere. And he'd built his fire in a shallow coulee, as if that would keep the smoke from drifting high and far. You could hear the bawling of the cows a long way off too.

I picketed my horse in some brush and eased up to the rim of the coulee and hunkered down behind a chokecherry to have a look at him. I wanted him to be a stranger, or one of the small dirt ranchers from out beyond the Knob. But you don't always get what you want in this life—hell, no, you don't—and I didn't this time. He wasn't a drifter and he wasn't a dirt rancher. He was just who I figured the brand-blotter to be: young Cal Dennison.

He had a running iron heating in the fire and he was squatting alongside, smoking a quirly while he waited. Close by were a lean-shanked orange dun cowpony and two of my Four Dot cows that he'd hobbled with piggin strings. The cows were both young brindle heifers, good breeding stock.

The tip of the running iron was starting to turn red. Cal Dennison rotated it once, finished his smoke, and went to drag one of the heifers over near the fire. When he set to work with that iron, he had his back to where I was. The smell of singed hair came up sharp on the warm afternoon breeze.

I stood and drew my Colt sixgun. Off on my left there was an easy path into the coulee. I moved there and made my way down, slow and careful. The bawling of the heifers covered what sounds I made. I stopped a dozen paces behind and to one side of him, close enough to see that he was almost done turning my Four Dot brand into a solid bar. If I gave him enough time he'd burn a "D" above the bar, the way he had with other of my cows over the past week or so. Then he'd do the other heifer and afterwards herd both over onto D-Bar graze, next to mine on the other side of Little Creek. D-Bar was Lyle Dennison's brand.

But I didn't give him enough time. I put the Colt's hammer on cock and said fast and loud, "You're caught, boy. Set still where you are."

He must have heard the snicking of the hammer because he was already moving by the time I got the words out. Cat-quick, he came all the way around with a look of wild surprise on his face.

"I said set still! You want to die, boy?"

Sight of the Colt and the tone of my voice, if not the words themselves, finally froze him on one knee with the running iron still in his hand. I could have emptied the Colt into him by the time he dropped the iron and drew his own sidearm, and he knew it. I watched him wet his mouth, get hold of himself; watched the wildness smooth out into an expression of sullen defiance.

"Bennett," he said, the way most men would say "Horseshit."

"Put the iron down. Slow."

He did it.

"Now your sixgun, even slower. Just two fingers."

He did that too.

"Untie the heifer. Then go do the same with the other one."

It took him a minute or so to get the piggin strings off the first heifer's legs. She scrambled up and went loping away down the coulee, still bawling. He got the second cow untied in quicker time, and while that one ran off he stood hipshot, glaring at me. I'd seen him in Cricklewood a few times but the Dennisons and the Bennetts had kept their distance the past twenty years; this was the first I'd had a good look at the boy up close. He'd be past nineteen now. Tall and sinewy and fair-skinned—the image of his ma, I thought. Same light brown curls and dark smoky eyes and proud stance. How long had Ellen Dennison been dead? Ten years? Eleven? Funny how time distorts your sense of its passage, how single years among all the long years blend and blur together until you can't tell one from another . . .

"Well?" young Cal said. "Now what?"

I didn't answer him. Instead I moved over to where he'd been by the fire and kicked his sidegun, an old Allen & Wheelock Navy .36, in among the branches of a wild rose bush.

He said angrily, "What'd you do that for? Them thorns'll scratch hell out of it."

"You won't be using it again."

"You going to shoot me, Bennett?"

"Mister Bennett to you."

"Go to hell, *Mister* Bennett."

"This was twenty years ago, I'd have already shot you."

"Well, it ain't twenty years ago."

"Rustling can still get you hung in this county."

"I ain't afraid of that. Or you, *Mister* Bennett."

"Then you're a damn fool in more ways than one."

He tried to work his mouth up into a sneer but he couldn't quite bring it off. He wasn't near so tough or fearless as he was trying to make out. His gaze shifted away from me, roved up along the rim of the coulee. "Where's the rest of your crew?"

"There's just me. I don't need a crew to run down one punk brand-blotter. Only took me a day and a half."

He had nothing to say to that.

I said, "How many of my cows have you burned?"

"You're so goddamn smart, you figure it out."

"My riders say at least half a dozen."

"Two thousand," he said, smart-mouth.

"All right, then. Your pa know what you been up to?"

". . . No."

"I didn't think so. Whatever else Lyle Dennison is, he's not a brand-burner and a cow thief."

"I'll tell you what he is," the boy said. "He's twice the man *you* are."

"Maybe so. But you're not half the man either of us ever was."

That flared up his anger again. "You stole three thousand acres that belonged to him! You turned him into a broken-down dirt rancher!"

"No. That land belonged to me. Circuit judge said so in open court—"

"You bought that judge! You bribed him! That's always been your way, *Mister* Bennett. Get what you want any way you can—lie and steal and cheat to get it. Ain't that right?"

There was another lie on my tongue, but it tasted bitter and I didn't say it. What did he know about how it was in the old days, a kid like him? Those three thousand acres were mine by right of first possession; my cattle were on free range before Lyle Dennison and others like him showed up in this valley. A man has to fight for what belongs to him, even if it means fighting dirty. If he doesn't, he loses it—and once it's gone, he'll never get it back. It's gone for good.

"That's what this brand-blotting business is all about?" I asked him. "Something that happened between your pa and me twenty years ago?"

"Damn right that's what it's all about. Way I figure it, I got as much right to steal your cattle as you had to steal my pa's land."

"Twenty years is a long time, boy. More years than you been on this earth."

"That don't change the way it was. Pa never would do nothing about it, he just give up. But not me. It's my fight now and I ain't giving up until it's settled, one way or another."

"Why is it your fight now?"

"Because it is."

"Something happen to your pa?"

"That's none of your look-out."

"You've made it my look-out. He didn't pass on, did he?"

". . . Might as well have."

"Sick, then? Some kind of ailment?"

The boy was silent for a time. But I could see it eating at him, the pain and the rage and the hate; he had to let it come out or bust from it. When he did let it come he threw the words at me as if they were knives. "He had a stroke last week. Crippled him. He can't hardly move, can't hardly talk, just lies there in his bed. You satisfied now? That make you happy?"

"No, boy, it doesn't. I'm sorry."

"Sorry? Christ—sorry! You son of a bitch—"

"That's enough. Go get your horse."

"What?"

"Get your horse. Lead him up to where mine is picketed."

"You takin' me to town?"

"We're going to the D-Bar. I want to see your pa."

"No!"

"You don't have a say in it. Do what I told you."

"Why? You aim to tell him about this?"

"Maybe. Maybe not."

"You do and it'll kill him."

"You should have thought of that before you came onto my land with that running iron."

"I won't go."

"You'll go," I said. "Sitting your saddle or tied across it with a bullet in your leg, either way."

He didn't move until I waggled the Colt at him. Then he spat hard into the grass and swung around and stomped over to where the orange dun was picketed.

Following him and the horse up to the coulee rim, I tried to figure what had put the notion to do this in my head. It wasn't just the brand-blotting. And it wasn't because I wanted to mortify the boy in front of Lyle, or that I wanted to pour salt in old wounds. Could be I would tell Lyle about the rustling but more likely I wouldn't. Maybe it was because Lyle Dennison and me had been friends once and now he was ailing, likely dying. Maybe it was that young Cal needed to be taught some kind of lesson. Or maybe it was just that there was a crazy need in me to touch the past again.

A man doesn't always know why he does a thing. Or need to know, for that matter. It's just something he has to do, so he goes ahead and does it. Let it go at that.

It was mid-afternoon when we came in sight of the D-Bar ranch buildings. They were grouped in a hollow where Little Creek ran, with the gaunt, snow-rimmed shapes of the Rockies rising up in the distance. I'd expected changes after so many years but none like the ones I saw as we topped the hill above the creek. The place appeared run-down, withered, as if nobody lived there any more. Gaps in the walls of the hip-roofed barn, missing rails in the corral fence, a rusty-wire chicken coop where the bunkhouse had once stood. The main house needed whitewash and new siding and a new roof. There had been flower beds and a vegetable garden once; now there were a few dried-up vines and bushes here and there, like scattered bones in a graveyard.

Cal said, "You like what you see, *Mister* Bennett?" and I come to realize he'd been watching me take it all in. It was the first he'd spoken since we had left my land.

"Why haven't you and your pa kept things up?"

"Why? Why in hell you think? He's old and I ain't got but two hands and there ain't but twenty-four hours in a day."

"Nobody working for you?"

"Not since anthrax took most of our cows two years ago."

"Anthrax took some of my cows too," I said.

"Sure it did. But then you went right out and bought some more, didn't you?"

We rode the rest of the way in a new silence. The boy leaned down and pulled the wooden pin that held the sagging gates shut, and we went on across the yard. Even the grass that grew here, even the big shade cottonwoods behind the house and the willows along the creek, seemed to have a dusty, lifeless look.

We drew rein at the tie rail near the house and got down. I said then, "I'll see him alone."

"Hell you will! You go waltzin' in there like you owned the place, he'll have another stroke—"

"You got no say in this, boy. I told you that."

"You can't just bust in on him!"

"I'll announce myself first."

"What about me? You expect me to just stand here and wait for you?"

"That's just what I expect. You won't run. And you won't try fighting me, neither, not with your pa lying in there."

We locked gazes; there was as much heat in it as a couple of maverick steers locking horns. But I was older and tougher and I had a sixgun besides, holstered though it was now and had been for most of the ride. Cal knew it as well as I did. It was what made him look away first, hating himself for doing it and hating me all the harder for backing him down.

He said thickly, "You goin' to tell him?"

"Still haven't made up my mind."

"He'll call you a liar if you do."

I said, "Stand here where you can hear me if I call you," and went on up the stairs to the screen door. He didn't try to follow me. When I turned to glance back at him he was rooted to the same spot with the hate shining out of his eyes like light shining out of a red-eye lantern.

I opened the screen door—the inside door was already open—and called, "Lyle? It's Sam Bennett. I've come to talk."

No answer.

"Sing out if you object to my coming in."

Still no answer.

I moved inside, let the screen door bang shut behind me. The day's warmth lay thick in the parlor. Dust, too—a thin layer of it on the floor and on the old, worn furniture. Ellen Dennison had been a neat, clean woman; she would have kept house the same way. But she was long gone. For ten or eleven years now it had been just Lyle and the boy.

"Lyle?"

My voice seemed to come bouncing back at me off the walls. I walked across the room, into a hall with three doors opening off of it. He was beyond the last of them, in the back bedroom. Lying in a four-poster with an old patchwork quilt draped over him. His eyes were wide open. One look at them that way and I knew he was dead.

One thin, veined hand lay palm up on the quilt. I went over and touched it, and it was cool and stiff. The stiffness was in his face and body too. Dead a while, since sometime this morning.

For a time I stood looking down at him. We were the same age, forty-six, but the years had ravaged him where they had only eroded me some. His hair was thin and gray-white, there were lines in his face as deep as cracks in sun-dried mud, and his hands were the hands of a man in his sixties. Death, for him, had come as something of a mercy.

A sadness built in me, seeing him up close like this, newly passed on. I'd never hated Lyle Dennison. He had been my friend once, and then he'd been my enemy, but I had never hated or even disliked him much. I'd hardly thought about him at all after the court fight. Hell, why should I? I'd claimed the three thousand acres and they were what counted. Land and money and power were the only things that counted.

That was the way I'd thought back then and most of my life, anyhow. It wasn't the way I thought now.

I leaned down to close Lyle's eyes. Then I made my way back through the house and out onto the porch. Cal was standing where I'd left him. The only thing he'd done was to take out the makings and build himself a smoke.

He said around the quirly, "That was some short talk."

"He's dead, Cal," I said.

"What?"

"Your pa is dead. Passed away this morning sometime, looks like."

"You're a goddamn liar!"

"Go in and see for yourself."

The cigarette dropped out of his mouth, hit the front of his hickory shirt and showered sparks on the way to the ground. He didn't notice. His face had gone bloodless. "You told him about me. You told him and he had another stroke—"

"He had another stroke, right enough. But he's been gone for hours. Go on, boy. See for yourself."

He bolted for the stairs. I got out of the way as he ran up and yanked open the screen door and bulled inside. When the door banged shut again I walked on down to the tie rail and made a cigarette of my own. But it tasted bad, like I was sucking in sulphur smoke; I threw it away after two drags. Then I just stood there and watched a hawk glide above the cottonwoods along the creek, and waited.

It was close to ten minutes before Cal came back out. By then he had himself under a tight rein, likely so I wouldn't see how much he was grieving. He came down to where I was and looked at me for a space, with the hate in his eyes banked now, smouldering.

He said, "Something I want to know."

"Ask it."

"If he'd been alive, would you of told him?"

"No," I said.

"How come?"

"This business is between you and me. You said as much yourself, back in the coulee."

He seemed to understand, or thought he did. He nodded once. "I'm goin' into town now, talk to the preacher and the undertaker. You can tell Sheriff Gaiters I'll be one place or the other when he wants me."

"What makes you think I'll be talking to Sheriff Gaiters?"

That surprised him some. "Mean you won't?"

"Not this time. But you stay off my land from now on. I catch you there again, or find out about any more brand-blotting, you'll pay and pay dear. You hear me?"

"I hear you," he said. "But you better hear something too, *Mister* Bennett. This don't change nothing. Nothing at all."

"I didn't expect it would."

"Just so you know. I ain't my pa's son. I ain't givin' up the way he did, never mind what you say or do."

He turned on his heel and walked over to the corral fence. Stood there with his back to me, gazing out at the mountains jutting sharp against the wide Montana sky, waiting for me to leave first.

I swung into leather, walked the horse slow across the yard. Cal moved his head to watch me. And I wondered again if I could shoot him, should it ever come down to that—kill him even in self-defense. Maybe, maybe not. You never know what you're capable of doing until the time comes for you to make a choice.

I wondered, too, if his ma had ever told Lyle about her and me. How I'd turned away from her in her time of need, because I was still wild and wanted no part of marriage and a family just then. How *her* choice, the only reasonable one open to her, had been to cast aside her pride and go straight to another man who did want to marry her. Not that it made a difference if she had told Lyle, for neither of them had ever told the boy. Nor would I, no matter what might happen between Cal and me. He had enough hate running through him as it was.

"I ain't my pa's son," the boy had said. But God help him, he was. In every way that counted he was just like his pa.

If a man doesn't fight for what belongs to him, he loses it. And once it's gone, he'll never get it back through all the long, empty years. It's gone for good. . . .

Decision

THE DAY WAS coming on dusk, the sky flame-streaked and the thick desert heat easing some, when I found the small hardscrabble ranch.

It lay nestled within a broad ring of bluffs and cactus-strewn hillocks. Crouched beside a draw leading between two of the bluffs was a pole-and-'dobe cabin and two weathered outbuildings. Even from where I sat my steeldust high above, I could see that whoever lived there was not having an easy time of it. Heat had parched and withered the corn and other vegetables in the cultivated patch along one side, and the spare buildings looked to be crumbling, like the powdering bones of animals long dead.

There were no horses or other livestock in the open corral near the cabin, no sign of life anywhere. Except for the wisps of chimney smoke rising pale and steady, the place had the look of abandonment. It was the smoke that had drawn me off El Camino Real del Diablo some minutes earlier; that and the fact that both my waterbags were near empty.

Most days there seemed to be a fair amount of traffic on the Devil's Highway—the only good road between Tucson and Yuma, part of the Gila Trail that connected California with points east to Texas. Over the past week I'd come on pioneers, freighters, drifters, a Butterfield stagecoach, a company of soldiers on its way to Fort Yuma, groups of men looking for work on the rail line the Southern Pacific had begun building eastward from the Colorado River the previous year, 1878. But

DECISION

today, when I needed water and would have paid dear for it, the road had been deserted.

It was my own fault that I was low on water. I could have filled the bags when I passed through the town of Maricopa Wells last night, but I'd decided to keep on without stopping; it had been late enough so that even the saloons were closed, and I saw no need to go knocking on someone's door at that hour. It was my intention to buy water at the next way station for the Butterfield line, but when I got there, close to noon, the stationmaster had refused me. His main spring had gone bad, he said, and they had precious little for their own needs. He'd let me stay there for most of the afternoon, waiting in the shade by the corral; not a soul had passed by the time I rode on again at five o'clock. And I had seen no one since, either.

I hoped the people who lived down below had enough water to spare. If they didn't I would have to go back to the Devil's Highway and do some more waiting; neither the steeldust nor I was fit enough for moving on without water. I could see the ranch's well set under a plank lean-to in the dusty yard and I licked at my parched lips. Well, I had nothing to lose by riding down and asking.

I heeled the horse forward, sitting slack in the saddle. Even traveling mostly by night, and even though it was not yet the middle of May, a man dries out in the desert, wearies bone-deep.

But the desert also had a way of dulling the mind, which was just the reason why I had decided to ride alone instead of traveling by coach through these Arizona badlands. I didn't want company or conversation because they would only lead to questions and then sharpened memories I did not care to dwell on. Memories that needed to be buried, the way I had buried Emma four months and six days ago in the sun-webbed ground outside Lordsburg.

People I knew there, friends, said the pain would go away

DECISION

after a while. All you had to do was to keep on living the best you could and time would help you forget—forget how she'd collapsed one evening after a dozen hours' hard toil on our own hardscrabble land, and how I'd thought it was just the ague because she'd been complaining of chest pains, and that terrible time when I came back from town with the doctor and found her lying in our bed so still and small, not breathing, gone. Heart failure, the doctor said. Twenty-eight years old, prime of life, and her good heart had betrayed her. . . .

Maybe they were right, the friends who'd given their advice. But four months and six days of living the best I could hadn't eased the grief inside me, not with everything and everyone in Lordsburg reminding me of Emma. So a week ago I had sold the farm, packed a few changes of clothing and some personal belongings and a spare pistol into my saddlebags, and set out west into Arizona Territory. I had no idea where I was going or what I would do when the three hundred and eighty dollars I carried in my boot dwindled away. I had nothing and I wanted nothing except to drift through the long days and longer nights until life took on some meaning again, if it ever would.

The trail leading down to the ranch was steep and switchbacked in places, and it took me the better part of twenty minutes to get to where the buildings were. The harsh daylight had softened by then and the tops of the bluffs seemed to have turned a reddish-purple color; the sky looked flushed now, instead of brassy the way it did at midday.

I rode slowly toward the cabin, keeping my hands up and in plain sight. Desert settlers, being as isolated as they were, would likely be mistrustful of leaned-down, dust-caked strangers. When I reached the front yard I drew rein. It was quiet there and I still wasn't able to make out sound or movement at any of the buildings. Beyond the vegetable patch, a sagging utility shed stood with a padlock on its door; the only other structure was a long pole-sided shelter at the rear of the empty corral. In back of the shed, rows of pulque cactus stood like sentinels in the hot, dry earth.

I looked at the well, running my tongue through the dryness inside my mouth. Then I eased the steeldust half a rod closer to the cabin and called out, "Hello the house!"

Silence.

"Hello! Anybody home?"

There was more silence for a couple of seconds, and I was thinking of stepping down. But then a woman's voice said from inside, "What do you want here?" It was a young voice, husky, but dulled by something I couldn't identify. The door was closed and the front window was curtained in monk's cloth, but I sensed that the woman was standing by the window, watching me through the curtain folds.

"Don't be alarmed, ma'am," I said. "I was wondering if you could spare a little water. I'm near out."

She didn't answer. Silence settled again, and I began to get a vague feeling of something being wrong. It made me shift uncomfortably in the saddle.

"Ma'am?"

"I can't let you have much," she said finally.

"I'll pay for whatever you can spare."

"You won't need to pay."

"That's kind of you."

"You can step down if you like."

I put on a smile and swung off and slapped some of the fine powdery dust off my shirt and Levi's. The door opened a crack, but she didn't come out.

"My name is Jennifer Todd," she said from inside. "My husband and I own this ranch." She spoke the word "husband" as if it were a blasphemy.

"I'm Roy Boone," I said.

"Mr. Boone." And she opened the door and moved out into the fading light.

DECISION

My smile vanished; I stared at her with my mouth coming open. She was no more than twenty, hair the color of near-ripe corn and piled in loose braids on top of her head, eyes brown and soft and wide—pretty eyes. But it wasn't any of this that caused me to stare as I did. It was the blue-black bruises on both sides of her face, the deep cut above her right brow, the swollen, mottled surface of her upper lip and her right temple.

"Jesus God!" I said. "Who did that to you, Mrs. Todd?"

"My husband. This morning, just before he left for Maricopa Wells."

"But *why*?"

"He was hung over," she said. "Pulque hung over. Mase is mean when he's sober and meaner when he's drunk, but when he's bad hung over he's the devil's own child."

"He's done this to you before?"

"More times than I can count."

"Maybe I've got no right to say this, but why don't you leave him? Mrs. Todd, a man who'd do a thing like this to a woman wouldn't hesitate to kill her if he was riled enough."

"I tried to leave him," she said. "I tried it three times. He came after me each time and brought me back here and beat me half crazy. A work animal's got sense enough to obey if it's whipped enough times."

I could feel anger inside me. I was thinking of Emma again, the love we'd had, the tenderness. Some men never knew or understood feelings like that; some men gave only one kind of pain, never felt the other kind deep inside them. They never realized what they had with a good woman. Or cared. Men like that—

Impulsively I put the rest of the thought into words. "A man like that ought to be shot dead for what he's done to you."

Something flickered in her eyes and she said, "If I had a gun, Mr. Boone, I expect I'd do just that thing—I'd shoot him, with no regrets. But there's only one rifle and one pistol, and

Mase carries them with him during the day. At night he locks them up in the shed yonder."

It made me feel uneasy to hear a woman talking so casually about killing. I looked away from her, wondering if it was love or some other reason that made her marry this Mase Todd, somebody who kept her like a prisoner in a badlands valley, who beat her and tried to break her.

When I looked back at Mrs. Todd she smiled in a fleeting, humorless way. "I don't know what's the matter with me, telling you all my troubles. You've problems of your own, riding alone across the desert. Come inside. I've some stew on the fire and you can take an early supper with me if you like."

"Ma'am, I—"

"Mase won't be home until late tonight or tomorrow morning, if you're thinking of him."

"I wasn't, no. He doesn't worry me."

"You look tired and hungry," she said, "and we don't get many visitors out here. I've no one to talk to most days. I'd take it as a kindness if you'd accept."

I couldn't find a way to refuse her. I just nodded and let her show me inside the cabin.

It was filled with shadows and smelled of spiced jackrabbit stew and boiling coffee. The few pieces of furniture were handhewn, but whoever had made them—likely her husband—had done a poor, thoughtless job; none of the pieces looked as though it would last much longer. But the two rooms I saw were clean and straightened, and you could see that she'd done the best she could with what she had, that she'd tried to make a home out of it.

She lighted a mill lantern on the table to chase away some of the shadows. Then she said, "There's water in that basin by the hearth if you want to wash up. I'll fetch some drinking water from the well, and I'll see to your horse."

"You needn't bother yourself . . ."

"It's no bother."

She turned and went to the door, walking in a stiff, slow way but holding herself erect; her spirit wasn't broken yet. I watched her go out and shut the door behind her, and I thought: She's some woman. Most would be half-dead shells by now if they'd gone through what she has.

I crossed to the basin, washed with a cake of strong yellow soap. Mrs. Todd came back as I was drying off. She handed me a gourd of water, and while I drank from it she unhooked a heavy iron kettle from a spit rod suspended above a banked fire. She spooned stew onto tin plates, poured coffee, set out a pan of fresh corn bread.

We ate mostly in silence. Despite what she'd said about not having anyone to talk to, she seemed not to want conversation. But there was something I needed to say, and when I was done eating I got it said.

"Mrs. Todd, you've been more than hospitable to share your food and water with me. I can't help feeling there must be something I can do for you."

"No, Mr. Boone. There's nothing you can do."

"Well, suppose I just stayed until your husband gets home, had a little talk with him—"

"That wouldn't be wise," she said. "If Mase comes home and finds a strange man, he wouldn't wait to ask who you are or why you're here. He'd make trouble for you, and afterward he'd make more trouble for me."

What could I do? It was her property, her life; this was business between her and her husband. If she'd asked for help, that would have been another matter. But she'd made her position clear. I had no right to force myself on her.

Outside, in the silky moon-washed purple of early evening, I thanked her again and tried to offer her money for the food and water. But she wouldn't have any of it. She was too proud to take payment for hospitality. She insisted that I fill my waterbags from the well before riding out, so I lowered the wooden bucket on the windlass and did that.

As I rode slowly out of the yard, I turned in the saddle to look back. She was still standing there by the well, looking after me, her hands down at her sides. In the silvery moonlight she had a forlorn, fixed appearance—as if she had somehow taken root in the desert soil.

An hour later I was once again on the Devil's Highway, headed west. And a mounting sense of uneasiness had come to ride with me. For the first time in four months and six days, it was someone other than Emma who was disturbing my thoughts; it was Jennifer Todd.

Like an echo in my mind, I heard some of the words she had spoken to me: *If I had a gun, Mr. Boone, I expect I'd do just that thing—I'd shoot him, with no regrets. But there's only one rifle and one pistol, and Mase carries them with him during the day.*

I listened to the echo of those words, and I thought about the way she'd been watching me inside the cabin when I first rode in, the way she'd suddenly opened the door and come outside. Why had she come out at all? Beaten the way she was, most women would have stayed in the privacy of the cabin rather than allow a stranger to see them that way. And why had she talked so freely about her husband, about the kind of man he was?

Then I heard other words she'd spoken—*I'll fetch some drinking water from the well, and I'll see to your horse*—and I drew sharp rein, swung quickly out of the saddle. My fingers fumbled at the straps on the saddlebags, pulled them open, groped inside.

My spare sixgun was missing.

And along with it, three or four cartridges.

I stood there in the moonlight, leaning against the steel-dust's flank, and I knew exactly what she had begun planning when she saw me ride in, and what she was planning for when her husband came home from Maricopa Wells and tried to lay hand on her again. And yet, I couldn't raise anger for what she'd done. She had been driven to it. She had every right to protect herself.

But was it really self-defense? Or was it cold-blooded murder?

In the saddle again, I thought: I've got to stop her. Only then Emma came crowding into my thoughts again. Gone, now—gone too young. So many years never to be lived, so many things never to be done; the child we had tried so hard to have never to be born. There had been nothing I could do to save her. But there was something I could do for another suffering young woman on another hardscrabble ranch.

I made my decision.

I kept on riding west.

Cave of Ice
(with Marcia Muller)

On the hottest day of summer in the year 1905, Will Reese disobeyed his father's orders and returned to the ice cave. He just couldn't stay away any longer. He had thought about little else but the cave for the past week.

The entrance was at the bottom of a deep, rock-strewn depression on his folks' sheep ranch, one of many such pits in this section of the southern Idaho plain. His father had told him they were collapsed lava cones that had been formed by long-ago flows from the extinct volcano nearby. As Will climbed down the depression, the temperature dropped with amazing swiftness. At the bottom, near the cave opening, the air had a wintry feel. The coldness was what had led him to the cave that day the previous week, after he had come here on the trail of a stray Hampshire yearling.

Will donned his sheepskin coat, lit the lantern he had brought, and wedged his tall, lanky frame through the fissure into the cave's main chamber. When he stood up, the light reflected in dazzling pinpoints from a hundred icy surfaces.

Ice filled the cave, from frozen pools along its floor to huge crystals suspended from its ceiling twenty feet above. A massive glacial wall bulked up directly ahead, a wall that might have been a few feet or many yards thick. Several natural stone steps, sheeted with ice, led up to a narrow ledge nearby. On the ledge's far side was an icefall, a natural slide that dropped fifteen feet into an arched lava tube. At the bottom of the slide was a jumble of gleaming bones, probably those of a large animal that had fallen down the slide and been unable to climb out.

Will could see his breath misting frostily in the lamplight. He could hear water dripping into the cave from underground streams, water that would soon be frozen. He felt the same excitement he had the first time he'd stood here. An ice cave! He hadn't known such things existed. But his father had; Clay Reese had an unquenchable thirst for knowledge, which he tried to slake by reading and rereading mail-order books on many different subjects. He had told Will about the caves, after Will had raced home with news of his find and brought his father back.

There were two kinds of ice caves, one type found in glaciers and the other in volcanic fissures such as this one. Usually the ice in both types melted in warm weather; but this was one of the rare exceptions. No one knew for sure how or why such caves acted as natural icehouses. Perhaps it had something to do with air pressure and wind flow. The phenomenon was very rare, which made Will's discovery all the more special to him.

His father, however, hadn't seemed to understand this. "I don't want you coming back here again," he'd said. "Now don't argue, Son. It's not safe in a cave like this; all kinds of things can happen. Stay clear."

Will had tried in vain to get his father to change his mind. Clay Reese was sometimes difficult to talk to, and lately he had been even more reticent than usual, as if something were weighing on his mind. A fiercely proud man, he had once dreamed of attending college, a dream that had ended with the death of his own father when he was Will's age, 15. Disappointment and hard work had turned him into a private person.

Yet he and Will had always shared a closeness based on fairness and understanding. Until now, he had always listened to Will's side of things. Will just didn't understand the sudden change in him.

Will spent the better part of an hour exploring. Between the ice wall and the near lava wall was a passage that led more than fifty yards deeper under the volcanic rock, before it ended finally in a glacial barrier that completely filled the cave. Small chambers formed by arches and broken-rock walls opened off the passage. The cave was enormous, no telling yet just how large.

But an hour was all he could spare. He would be missed if he stayed much longer, and he had already been reprimanded more than once this week for neglecting his chores. He made his way back to the main chamber and slipped outside, shrugging out of his coat.

The summer heat was intense after the cave's chill; Will was sweating by the time he reached the rim of the pit. He started toward where he had left his roan horse picketed in the shade of a lava overhang. But then he stopped and stood shading his eyes, peering out over the flat, sun-blasted plain.

Billows of dust rose in a long line, hazing the bright blue sky. Wagons, four of them, were coming from the direction of Volcano, the only settlement within twenty miles. They weren't traveling on the road that led out among the sheep ranches in the area; they were coming at an angle through the sagebrush. And they seemed to be heading toward Will.

Frowning, he moved over next to his horse and waited there, hidden, holding the animal's muzzle to keep him still. The wagons clattered ahead without changing course and finally drew to a halt at the far end of the pit, where it was easiest to scale the rocky wall. Close to a dozen men clambered down and began to unload lumber, a keg of nails, coils of rope, axes, picks, shovels, and other tools.

Stunned, Will saw that one of the men was his father. Clay Reese, in fact, seemed to be directing the activities of the others. Will also recognized Jess Lacy, proprietor of the Volcano Mercantile, and Harmon Bennett, president of the bank. The other men were laborers.

"First thing to do," Will heard his father say, "is clear a path into the pit so we can take the wagons down there. We'll also have to enlarge the cave opening."

"Dynamite, Clay?" one of the men asked.

"No. Picks and shovels should do it. Then we can start building the ramps and cutting the ice into blocks."

Along with Jess Lacy and Harmon Bennett, Clay Reese disappeared inside the cave. The other men began clearing away rocks, grading a pathway for the wagons.

Will had seen enough. He led the roan away quietly, then mounted and rode out across the plain. His shock had given way to a sense of betrayal.

The town could use ice on these scorching summer days, when cellars weren't able to preserve meat and other perishables; Will understood that. But what he didn't understand was why his father had kept secret his decision to sell the ice. The cave belonged to Will more than to anybody, because *he* had found it. So why hadn't his father told him what he intended to do?

Will decided to ask him at dinner.

He rode out to the ranch's north boundary fence to make one of three repairs he had been asked to attend to. By the time he finished it was too late to make the others; the sun was just starting to wester. He rode on home.

The ranch wagon stood in front of the weathered barn when he arrived, but his father's saddle horse was gone. So were two of the family's three sheep dogs. The other dog followed him into the barn, its barks mingling with the bleating of the sheep in the pens that flanked the shearing shed. He unsaddled his roan, fed it some hay, then crossed to the small sod house under the cottonwoods and went inside.

His mother, in spite of it being the hottest day of the year, was stirring a stewpot on the back iron stove. She turned, her eyes stern. "Will, where have you been all day?"

"I . . . Where's Pa?"

"Out east. A ewe and her lamb got through that fence you were supposed to mend and fell into one of the lava pits. Honestly, Will, I don't know what's the matter with you lately. Your father shouldn't have to attend to your chores."

Clay Reese returned an hour before sundown. Immediately he called Will outside and reprimanded him for neglecting to mend the east fence. "The ewe and her lamb weren't badly hurt," he said, "but they might have been killed."

"I'm sorry, Pa."

His father grunted and started to turn away.

"Pa," Will said, "I was at the ice cave today. I saw you come out with the men from town."

"What? I thought I told you not to go there!"

"Yes, sir, you did. But why didn't you tell me you planned to sell the ice?"

"Because it's not your business, that's why."

"Pa, it *is* my business. I found that cave. And we've always talked about things before."

"That's enough!" Clay Reese's lean face was flushed. "We won't discuss it. You stay away from that cave. Understood?"

"Yes, sir."

Baffled and hurt, Will tried to bring the subject up again the next day. But his father once more refused to discuss it. Will went about his chores, a sad, empty feeling growing inside him.

Ever since he'd been small, his father had treated him as an adult. The ranch was not a prosperous one, and all three Reeses worked in partnership to keep it going. Yet now his father was shutting him out, and it hurt; it was making him lose respect for a man he had always looked up to. Will couldn't bear that. He began to think of leaving the ranch, striking out on his own.

He could go to a city—Boise, perhaps—and find work. Then, later on, he could enter college, for his father's thirst for knowledge had been instilled in him too, and Clay Reese's dream had become his dream. He knew that leaving home would be a form of betrayal, but no more of one than his father's.

He determined to try one more time to talk to the man. It was Saturday noon, and thunderclouds were piling up in the east, when Will approached his father again. Clay Reese was hitching up the wagon for a drive somewhere.

"Pa," he said, "I have to talk to you about the ice cave."

His father's face seemed to cloud as darkly as the sky. "How many times do I have to tell you, Will? There's nothing to discuss. I can't talk now, anyway. I have business to attend to." He climbed into the wagon seat, flicked the reins and drove off.

Resigned, Will went to his room and packed a bundle. He would leave that night, after his parents were asleep.

The storm broke around 4 P.M., with thunder and lightning and gusty winds. Clay Reese did not return for supper, and finally Will and his mother ate without him. He had probably decided to wait out the storm in town.

Will spent a restless night as thunder grumbled and rain pelted. It would have been foolish to start his journey in this storm, and until his father returned, he didn't feel right leaving his mother alone.

Sometime toward morning the storm passed, and he fell into a heavy sleep. It was well past dawn, with the sun blazing again, when his mother awoke him. "Get up, Will," she said.

Her voice was anxious. "Your father still isn't home and I'm worried. You'd best ride into town and try to find him."

"Right away, Ma."

Will dressed quickly, saddled his roan and rode into the clear, rain-fresh morning. He'd only gone half a mile toward Volcano, however, when he thought of the cave. His father could have gone there yesterday, instead of to town; the ice might have been the business he'd referred to. And it wouldn't take long to check. Will turned his horse off the road and pointed him across open land.

He saw his father's wagon as soon as he came in sight of the lava pit.

He sent the roan into a hard run, reined up beside the wagon, and jumped off. There was no sign of Clay Reese, or of any of the laborers, this being Sunday. Will scrambled down the newly graded wagon ramp and ran to the cave opening. It had been enlarged considerably, shored up with timbers. He entered, fumbling in the pocket of his pants for matches.

In the flare of the first match he struck, he saw a jumble of equipment piled to one side; among the axes and picks and coiled rope was a lantern. He used a second match to light the lantern's wick. Now he could see more of the cave—gouges and holes in the once-smooth walls where ice blocks had been cut away; narrow wooden ramps built into the passageway, close to the floor, so that the blocks could be easily dragged out. But there was no sign of his father.

Carrying the lantern, Will hurried deeper into the cave. He went all the way to the solid barrier, then came back and checked some of the smaller chambers. All of them were empty.

He had to fight down panic as he ran back into the main chamber. His father *must* have come into the cave; where could he be? Then Will's gaze picked up the stone steps, the ledge at their top; and the chill air seemed to grow even colder. He climbed the steps, moving as fast as he dared on the slippery surface ice. When he reached the top, he leaned into the fall with the lantern extended.

Down at the bottom of the slide, a huddled form lay alongside the bones of the long-dead animal.

"Pa!" Will shouted the word, shouted it again. But the huddled figure didn't move.

Will half-ran, half-slid down the steps and got one of the coils of rope. Back on the ledge, he found a projection of rock and tied one end of the rope securely around it. He played the other end down the fall, tested the fastening, then swung his body onto the slide and let himself down to where his father lay.

Clay Reese was unconscious, but still alive. Will's relief didn't last long, however. Try as he might, he couldn't revive his father. The man had been here all night, lying on the ice. He seemed half-frozen. If he did regain consciousness, Will knew, he wouldn't have the strength to climb out by himself.

Will swiftly tied the rope around his father, under the arms. When he struggled back up to the ledge, he tried to pull his father out, but he didn't have the strength to move the inert figure more than a foot or so. He had to have help, yet if he left, his father might die before he could bring men back.

Then another idea came to him, and he wasted no time putting it into action. He got a second coil of rope from below, unfastened the first rope from the projection, and tied the two ropes together to make one long one. When he took the free end down across the cave and outside, he had 10 feet left.

He climbed to where the roan stood, caught the bridle and urged the animal to the cave's entrance. He tied the rope to the saddle horn, mounted, and backed the roan until the rope was taut. Then he and the horse began to pull.

It took agonizing minutes, the roan stumbling a time or two, almost losing balance. But finally the rope slackened somewhat, and this told Will his father had at last been drawn to the top of the fall. Dismounting, he raced back into the cave.

Clay Reese lay sprawled across the ledge. He was starting to regain consciousness when Will reached his side.

He managed to get his father to his feet, then down the steps, out of the cave, and to the far end of the pit where the day's heat penetrated. Exhausted, they both sank to the rocky ground. Clay Reese gave his son a weak smile.

"You saved my life," he said when the sun began to take away his chill. "I thought I was a dead man for sure."

"What happened, Pa?"

"I climbed those steps out of curiosity, slipped on the ice and fell down the slide. I couldn't get back out again." His expression turned rueful. "I told you it could be dangerous in there, Will; that you shouldn't go in alone. I should have obeyed my own orders."

"Why did you go in alone?"

"To do some exploring, see if I could tell how big the cave really is. If there's enough ice to last another couple of summers, I reckon we'll start making some money."

"*Start* making money?" Will asked, surprised.

"Will, you have a right to know the truth." His father spoke slowly, the words coming hard for him. "The reason I didn't talk to you about selling the ice is that I was afraid to face up to you. I didn't want anyone to know how close we were to losing the ranch. Until you found the cave, I hadn't been able to make the mortgage payments for some time; the bank was getting ready to foreclose."

"So that's why you've been so troubled lately."

"Yes. I worked out an arrangement with Jess Lacy, and with Harmon Bennett at the bank. Jess buys the ice at a fair price, and I turn the money over to Mr. Bennett. The mortgage will be paid off by next summer. Then we can start saving for your college education."

Will was silent for a time; he felt ashamed at having doubted his father. Finally he said, "Pa, I understand now. But I wish you'd told me all of this before."

"I guess I should have," his father admitted. "But my foolish pride wouldn't let me. I'm sorry, Son."

"I'm sorry too," Will said. "I . . . well, I felt like you didn't need me anymore. I was going to leave, go off to Boise and hunt work. I'd be gone now if it hadn't stormed last night."

His father grimaced, his face etched with pain. "This has been a bad misunderstanding, Will. From now on, we'll both be honest with each other. As for the cave, well, we'll explore it together next time. And work together on our ice business too."

"I'd like that, Pa."

Will stood and began to help his father up the ramp to the wagon. As he did, he glanced over at the mouth of the cave—not his cave, but the family's cave. Then his eyes met his father's, and they both smiled.

The Hanging Man

It was Sam McCullough who found the hanging man, down on the river bank behind his livery stable.

Straightaway he went looking for Ed Bozeman and me, being as we were the local sheriff's deputies. Tule River didn't have any fulltime law officers back then, in the late 1890s; just volunteers like Boze and me to keep the peace, and a fat-bottomed sheriff who came through from the county seat two or three days a month to look things over and to stuff himself on pig's knuckles at the Germany Café.

Time was just past sunup, on one of those frosty mornings Northern California gets in late November, and Sam found Boze already to work inside his mercantile. But they had to come fetch me out of my house, where I was just sitting down to breakfast. I never did open up my place of business—Miller's Feed and Grain—until 8:30 of a weekday morning.

I had some trouble believing it when Sam first told about the hanging man. He said, "Well, how in hell do you think *I* felt." He always has been an excitable sort and he was frothed up for fair just then. "I like to had a hemorrhage when I saw him hanging there on that black oak. Damnedest sight a man ever stumbled on."

"You say he's a stranger?"

"Stranger to me. Never seen him before."

"You make sure he's dead?"

Sam made a snorting noise. "I ain't even going to answer that. You just come along and see for yourself."

THE HANGING MAN

I got my coat, told my wife Ginny to ring up Doc Petersen on Mr. Bell's invention, and then hustled out with Sam and Boze. It was mighty cold that morning; the sky was clear and brittle-looking, like blue-painted glass, and the sun had the look of a two-day-old egg yolk above the tule marshes east of the river. When we came in alongside the stable I saw that there was silvery frost all over the grass on the river bank. You could hear it crunch when you walked on it.

The hanging man had frost on him, too. He was strung up on a fat old oak between the stable and the river, opposite a high board fence that separated Sam's property from Joel Pennywell's fixit shop next door. Dressed mostly in black, he was—black denims, black boots, a black cutaway coat that had seen better days. He had black hair, too, long and kind of matted. And a black tongue pushed out at one corner of a black-mottled face. All that black was streaked in silver, and there was silver on the rope that stretched between his neck and the thick limb above. He was the damnedest sight a man ever stumbled on, all right. Frozen up there, silver and black, glistening in the cold sunlight, like something cast up from the Pit.

We stood looking at him for a time, not saying anything. There was a thin wind off the river and I could feel it prickling up the hair on my neck. But it didn't stir that hanging man, nor any part of him or his clothing.

Boze cleared his throat, and he did it loud enough to make me jump. He asked me, "You know him, Carl?"

"No," I said. "You?"

"No. Drifter, you think?"

"Got the look of one."

Which he did. He'd been in his thirties, smallish, with a clean-shaven fox face and pointy ears. His clothes were shabby, shirt cuffs frayed, button missing off his cutaway coat. We got us a fair number of drifters in Tule River, up from San

Francisco or over from the mining country after their luck and their money ran out—men looking for farm work or such other jobs as they could find. Or sometimes looking for trouble. Boze and I had caught one just two weeks before and locked him up for chicken stealing.

"What I want to know," Sam said, "is what in the name of hell he's doing *here*?"

Boze shrugged and rubbed at his bald spot, like he always does when he's fuddled. He was the same age as me, thirty-four, but he'd been losing his hair for the past ten years. He said, "Appears he's been hanging a while. When'd you close up last evening, Sam?"

"Six, like always."

"Anybody come around afterwards?"

"No."

"Could've happened any time after six, then. It's kind of a lonely spot back here after dark. I reckon there's not much chance anybody saw what happened."

"Joel Pennywell, maybe," I said. "He stays open late some nights."

"We can ask him."

Sam said, "But why'd anybody string him up like that?"

"Maybe he wasn't strung up. Maybe he hung himself."

"Suicide?"

"It's been known to happen," Boze said.

Doc Petersen showed up just then, and a couple of other townsfolk with him; word was starting to get around. Doc, who was sixty and dyspeptic, squinted up at the hanging man, grunted, and said, "Strangulation."

"Doc?"

"Strangulation. Man strangled to death. You can see that from the way his tongue's out. Neck's not broken; you can see that too."

"Does that mean he could've killed himself?"

THE HANGING MAN

"All it means," Doc said, "is that he didn't jump off a high branch or get jerked hard enough off a horse to break his neck."

"Wasn't a horse involved anyway," I said. "There'd be shoe marks in the area; ground was soft enough last night, before the freeze. Boot marks here and there, but that's all."

"I don't know anything about that," Doc said. "All I know is, that gent up there died of strangulation. You want me to tell you anything else, you'll have to cut him down first."

Sam and Boze went to the stable to fetch a ladder. While they were gone I paced around some, to see if there was anything to find in the vicinity. And I did find something, about a dozen feet from the oak where the boot tracks were heaviest in the grass. It was a circlet of bronze, about three inches in diameter, and when I picked it up, I saw that it was one of those Presidential Medals the government used to issue at the Philadelphia Mint. On one side it had a likeness of Benjamin Harrison, along with his name and the date of his inauguration, 1889, and on the other were a tomahawk, a peace pipe, and a pair of clasped hands.

There weren't many such medals in California; mostly they'd been supplied to Army officers in other parts of the West, who handed them out to Indians after peace treaties were signed. But this one struck a chord in my memory: I recollected having seen it or one like it some months back. The only thing was, I couldn't quite remember where.

Before I could think any more on it, Boze and Sam came back with the ladder, a plank board, and a horse blanket. Neither of them seemed inclined to do the job at hand, so I climbed up myself and sawed through that half-frozen rope with my pocket knife. It wasn't good work; my mouth was dry when it was done. When we had him down we covered him up and laid him on the plank. Then we carried him out to Doc's wagon and took him to the Spencer Funeral Home.

After Doc and Obe Spencer stripped the body, Boze and I

went through the dead man's clothing. There was no identification of any kind; if he'd been carrying any before he died, somebody had filched it. No wallet or purse, either. All he had in his pockets was the stub of a lead pencil, a half-used book of matches, a short-six seegar, a nearly empty Bull Durham sack, three wheatstraw papers, a two-bit piece, an old Spanish *real* coin, and a dog-eared and stained copy of a Beadle dime novel called *Captain Dick Talbot, King of the Road; Or, The Black-Hoods of Shasta.*

"Drifter, all right," Boze said when we were done. "Wouldn't you say, Carl?"

"Sure seems that way."

"But even drifters have more belongings than this. Shaving gear, extra clothes—at least that much."

"You'd think so," I said. "Might be he had a carpetbag or the like and it's hidden somewhere along the river bank."

"Either that or it was stolen. But we can go take a look when Doc gets through studying on the body."

I fished out the bronze medal I'd found in the grass earlier and showed it to him. "Picked this up while you and Sam were getting the ladder," I said.

"Belonged to the hanging man, maybe."

"Maybe. But it seems familiar, somehow. I can't quite place where I've seen one like it."

Boze turned the medal over in his hand. "Doesn't ring any bells for me," he said.

"Well, you don't see many around here, and the one I recollect was also a Benjamin Harrison. Could be coincidence, I suppose. Must be if that fella died by his own hand."

"If he did."

"Boze, you think it *was* suicide?"

"I'm hoping it was," he said, but he didn't sound any more convinced than I was. "I don't like the thought of a murderer running around loose in Tule River."

"That makes two of us," I said.

Doc didn't have much to tell us when he came out. The hanging man had been shot once a long time ago—he had bullet scars on his right shoulder and back—and one foot was missing a pair of toes. There was also a fresh bruise on the left side of his head, above the ear.

Boze asked, "Is it a big bruise, Doc?"

"Big enough."

"Could somebody have hit him hard enough to knock him out?"

"And then hung him afterward? Well, it could've happened that way. His neck's full of rope burns and lacerations, the way it would be if somebody hauled him up over that tree limb."

"Can you reckon how long he's been dead?"

"Last night some time. Best I can do."

Boze and I headed back to the livery stable. The town had come awake by this time. There were plenty of people on the boardwalks and Main Street was crowded with horses and farm wagons; any day now I expected to see somebody with one of those newfangled motor cars. The hanging man was getting plenty of lip service, on Main Street and among the crowd that had gathered back of the stable to gawk at the black oak and trample the grass.

Nothing much goes on in a small town like Tule River, and such as a hanging was bound to stir up folks' imaginations. There hadn't been a killing in the area in four or five years. And damned little mystery since the town was founded back in the days when General Vallejo owned most of the land hereabouts and it was the Mexican flag, not the Stars and Stripes, that flew over California.

None of the crowd had found anything in the way of evidence on the river bank; they would have told us if they had. None of them knew anything about the hanging man, either. That included Joel Pennywell, who had come over from his fixit shop next door. He'd closed up around 6:30 last night, he said, and gone straight on home.

After a time Boze and I moved down to the river's edge and commenced a search among the tule grass and trees that grew along there. The day had warmed some; the wind was down and the sun had melted off the last of the frost. A few of the others joined in with us, eager and boisterous, like it was an Easter egg hunt. It was too soon for the full impact of what had happened to settle in on most folks; it hadn't occurred to them yet that maybe they ought to be concerned.

A few minutes before ten o'clock, while we were combing the west-side bank up near the Main Street Basin, and still not finding anything, the Whipple youngster came running to tell us that Roberto Ortega and Sam McCullough wanted to see us at the livery stable. Roberto owned a dairy ranch just south of town and claimed to be a descendant of a Spanish conquistador. He was also an honest man, which was why he was in town that morning. He'd found a saddled horse grazing on his pastureland and figured it for a runaway from Sam's livery, so he'd brought it in. But Sam had never seen the animal, an old swaybacked roan, until Roberto showed up with it. Nor had he ever seen the battered carpetbag that was tied behind the cantle of the cheap Mexican saddle.

It figured to be the drifter's horse and carpetbag, sure enough. But whether the drifter had turned the animal loose himself, or somebody else had, we had no way of knowing. As for the carpetbag, it didn't tell us any more about the hanging man than the contents of his pockets. Inside it were some extra clothes, an old Colt Dragoon revolver, shaving tackle, a woman's garter, and nothing at all that might identify the owner.

Sam took the horse, and Boze and I took the carpetbag over to Obe Spencer's to put with the rest of the hanging man's belongings. On the way we held a conference. Fact was, a pair of grain barges were due upriver from San Francisco at eleven, for loading and return. I had three men working for me, but none of them handled the paperwork; I was going to have to spend some time at the feed mill that day, whether I wanted to or not. Which is how it is when you have part-time deputies who are also full-time businessmen. It was a fact of small-town life we'd had to learn to live with.

We worked it out so that Boze would continue making inquiries while I went to work at the mill. Then we'd switch off at one o'clock so he could give his wife Ellie, who was minding the mercantile, some help with customers and with the drummers who always flocked around with Christmas wares right after Thanksgiving.

We also decided that if neither of us turned up any new information by five o'clock—or even if we did—we would ring up the country seat and make a full report to the sheriff. Not that Joe Perkins would be able to find out anything we couldn't. He was a fat-cat political appointee, and about all he knew how to find was pig's knuckles and beer. But we were bound to do it by the oath of office we'd taken.

We split up at the funeral parlor and I went straight to the mill. My foreman, Gene Kleinschmidt, had opened up; I'd given him a set of keys and he knew to go ahead and unlock the place if I wasn't around. The barges came in twenty minutes after I did, and I had to hustle to get the paperwork ready that they would be carrying back down to San Francisco—bills of lading, requisitions for goods from three different companies.

I finished up a little past noon and went out onto the dock to watch the loading. One of the bargemen was talking to Gene. And while he was doing it, he kept flipping something up and down in his hand—a small gold nugget. It was the kind of thing folks made into a watch fob, or kept as a good-luck charm.

And that was how I remembered where I'd seen the Benjamin Harrison Presidential Medal. Eight months or so back a newcomer to the area, a man named Jubal Parsons, had come in to buy some sacks of chicken feed. When he'd reached into his pocket to pay the bill he had accidentally come out with the medal. "Good-luck charm," he said, and let me glance at it before putting it away again.

Back inside my office I sat down and thought about Jubal Parsons. He was a tenant farmer—had taken over a small farm owned by the Siler brothers out near Willow Creek about nine months ago. Big fellow, over six feet tall, and upwards of 220 pounds. Married to a blonde woman named Greta, a few years younger than him and pretty as they come. Too pretty, some said; a few of the womenfolk, Ellie Bozeman included, thought she had the look and mannerisms of a tramp.

Parsons came into Tule River two or three times a month to trade for supplies, but you seldom saw the wife. Neither of them went to church on Sunday, nor to any of the social events at the Odd Fellows Hall. Parsons kept to himself mostly, didn't seem to have any friends or any particular vices. Always civil, at least to me, but taciturn and kind of broody-looking. Not the sort of fellow you find yourself liking much.

But did the medal I'd found belong to him? And if it did, had he hung the drifter? And if he had, what was his motive?

I was still puzzling on that when Boze showed up. He was a half hour early, and he had Floyd Jones with him. Floyd looked some like Santa Claus—fat and jolly and white-haired—and he liked it when you told him so. He was the night bartender at the Elkhorn Bar and Grill.

Boze said, "Got some news, Carl. Floyd here saw the hanging man last night. Recognized the body over to Obe Spencer's just now."

Floyd bobbed his head up and down. "He came into the Elkhorn about eight o'clock, asking for work."

I said, "How long did he stay?"

"Half hour, maybe. Told him we already had a swamper and he spent five minutes trying to convince me he'd do a better job of cleaning up. Then he gave it up when he come to see I wasn't listening, and bought a beer and nursed it over by the stove. Seemed he didn't much relish going back into the cold."

"He say anything else to you?"

"Not that I can recall."

"Didn't give his name, either," Boze said. "But there's something else. Tell him, Floyd."

"Well, there was another fella came in just after the drifter," Floyd said. "Ordered a beer and sat watching him. Never took his eyes off that drifter once. I wouldn't have noticed except for that and because we were near empty. Cold kept most everybody to home last night."

"You know this second man?" I asked.

"Sure do. Local farmer. Newcomer to the area, only been around for—"

"Jubal Parsons?"

Floyd blinked at me. "Now how in thunder did you know that?"

"Lucky guess. Parsons leave right after the drifter?"

"He did. Not more than ten seconds afterward."

"You see which direction they went?"

"Downstreet, I think. Toward Sam McCullough's livery."

I thanked Floyd for his help and shooed him on his way. When he was gone Boze asked me, "Just how did you know it was Jubal Parsons?"

"I finally remembered where I'd seen that Presidential Medal I found. Parsons showed it when he was here one day several months ago. Said it was his good-luck charm."

Boze rubbed at his bald spot. "That and Floyd's testimony make a pretty good case against him, don't they?"

"They do. Reckon I'll go out and have a talk with him."

"We'll both go," Boze said. "Ellie can mind the store the

rest of the day. This is more important. Besides, if Parsons *is* a killer, it'll be safer if there are two of us."

I didn't argue; a hero is something I never was nor wanted to be. We left the mill and went and picked up Boze's buckboard from behind the mercantile. On the way out of town we stopped by his house and mine long enough to fetch our rifles. Then we headed west on Willow Creek Road.

It was a long cool ride out to Jubal Parsons' tenant farm, through a lot of rich farmland and stands of willows and evergreens. Neither of us said much. There wasn't much to say. But I was tensed up and I could see that Boze was, too.

A rutted trail hooked up to the farm from Willow Creek Road, and Boze jounced the buckboard along there some past three o'clock. It was pretty modest acreage. Just a few fields of corn and alfalfa, with a cluster of ramshackle buildings set near where Willow Creek cut through the northwest corner. There was a one-room farmhouse, a chicken coop, a barn, a couple of lean-tos, and a pole corral. That was all except for a small windmill—a Fairbanks, Morse Eclipse—that the Siler brothers had put up because the creek was dry more than half the year.

When we came in sight of the buildings I could tell that Jubal Parsons had done work on the place. The farmhouse had a fresh coat of whitewash, as did the chicken coop, and the barn had a new roof.

There was nobody in the farmyard, just half a dozen squawking leghorns, when we pulled in and Boze drew rein. But as soon as we stepped down, the front door of the house opened and Greta Parsons came out on the porch. She was wearing a calico dress and high-button shoes, but her head was bare; that butter-yellow hair of hers hung down to her hips, glistening like the bargeman's gold nugget in the sun. She was some pretty woman, for a fact. It made your throat thicken up just to look at her, and funny ideas start to stir around in your head. If ever there was a woman to tempt a man to sin, I thought, it was this one.

Boze stayed near the buckboard, with his rifle held loose in one hand, while I went over to the porch steps and took off my hat. "I'm Carl Miller, Mrs. Parsons," I said. "That's Ed Bozeman back there. We're from Tule River. Maybe you remember seeing us?"

"Yes, Mr. Miller. I remember you."

"We'd like a few words with your husband. Would he be somewhere nearby?"

"He's in the barn," she said. There was something odd about her voice—a kind of dullness, as if she was fatigued. She moved that way, too, loose and jerky. She didn't seem to notice Boze's rifle, or to care if she did.

I said, "Do you want to call him out for us?"

"No, you go on in. It's all right."

I nodded to her and rejoined Boze, and we walked on over to the barn. Alongside it was a McCormick & Deering binder-harvester, and further down, under a lean-to, was an old buggy with its storm curtains buttoned up. A big gray horse stood in the corral, nuzzling a pile of hay. The smell of dust and earth and manure was ripe on the cool air.

The barn doors were shut. I opened one half, stood aside from the opening, and called out, "Mr. Parsons? You in there?"

No answer.

I looked at Boze. He said, "We'll go in together," and I nodded. Then we shouldered up and I pulled the other door half open. And we went inside.

It was shadowed in there, even with the doors open; those parts of the interior I could make out were empty. I eased away from Boze, toward where the corn crib was. There was sweat on me; I wished I'd taken my own rifle out of the buckboard.

"Mr. Parsons?"

Still no answer. I would have tried a third time, but right then Boze said, "Never mind, Carl," in a way that made me turn around and face him.

He was a dozen paces away, staring down at something under the hayloft. I frowned and moved over to him. Then I saw too, and my mouth came open and there was a slithery feeling on my back.

Jubal Parsons was lying there dead on the sod floor, with blood all over his shirtfront and the side of his face. He'd been shot. There was a .45-70 Springfield rifle beside the body, and when Boze bent down and struck a match, you could see the black-powder marks mixed up with the blood.

"My God," I said, soft.

"Shot twice," Boze said. "Head and chest."

"Twice rules out suicide."

"Yeah," he said.

We traded looks in the dim light. Then we turned and crossed back to the doors. When we came out Mrs. Parsons was sitting on the front steps of the house, looking past the windmill at the alfalfa fields. We went over and stopped in front of her. The sun was at our backs, and the way we stood put her in our shadow. That was what made her look up; she hadn't seen us coming, or heard us crossing the yard.

She said, "Did you find him?"

"We found him," Boze said. He took out his badge and showed it to her. "We're county sheriff's deputies, Mrs. Parsons. You'd best tell us what happened in there."

"I shot him," she said. Matter-of-fact, like she was telling you the time of day. "This morning, just after breakfast. Ever since I've wanted to hitch up the buggy and drive in and tell about it, but I couldn't seem to find the courage. It took all the courage I had to fire the rifle."

"But why'd you do a thing like that?"

"Because of what he did in Tule River last night."

"You mean the hanging man?"
"Yes. Jubal killed him."
"Did he tell you that?"
"Yes. Not long before I shot him."
"Why did he do it—hang that fellow?"
"He was crazy jealous, that's why."
I asked her, "Who was the dead man?"
"I don't know."
"You mean to say he was a stranger?"
"Yes," she said. "I only saw him once. Yesterday afternoon. He rode in looking for work. I told him we didn't have any, that we were tenant farmers, but he wouldn't leave. He kept following me around, saying things. He thought I was alone here—a woman alone."
"Did he—make trouble for you?"
"Just with words. He kept saying things, ugly things. Men like that—I don't know why, but they think I'm a woman of easy virtue. It has always been that way, no matter where we've lived."
"What did you do?" Boze asked.
"Ignored him at first. Then I begged him to go away. I told him my husband was wild jealous, but he didn't believe me. I thought I was alone too, you see; I thought Jubal had gone off to work in the fields."
"But he hadn't?"
"Oh, he had. But he came back while the drifter was here and he overheard part of what was said."
"Did he show himself to the man?"
"No. He would have if matters had gone beyond words, but that didn't happen. After a while he got tired of tormenting me and went away. The drifter, I mean."
"Then what happened?"
"Jubal saddled his horse and followed him. He followed that

man into Tule River and when he caught up with him he knocked him on the head and he hung him."

Boze and I traded another look. I said what both of us were thinking: "Just for deviling you? He hung a man for that?"

"I told you, Jubal was crazy jealous. You didn't know him. You just—you don't know how he was. He said that if a man thought evil, and spoke evil, it was the same as doing evil. He said if a man was wicked, he deserved to be hung for his wickedness and the world would be a better place for his leaving it."

She paused, and then made a gesture with one hand at her bosom. It was a meaningless kind of gesture, but you could see where a man might take it the wrong way. Might take *her* the wrong way, just like she'd said. And not just a man, either; women, too. Everybody that didn't keep their minds open and went rooting around after sin in other folks.

"Besides," she went on, "he worshipped the ground I stand on. He truly did, you know. He couldn't bear the thought of anyone sullying me."

I cleared my throat. The sweat on me had dried and I felt cold now. "Did you hate him, Mrs. Parsons?"

"Yes, I hated him. Oh, yes. I feared him, too—for a long time I feared him more than anything else. He was so big. And so strong-willed. I used to tremble sometimes, just to look at him."

"Was he cruel to you?" Boze asked. "Did he hurt you?"

"He was and he did. But not the way you mean; he didn't beat me, or once lay a hand to me the whole nine years we were married. It was his vengeance that hurt me. I couldn't stand it, I couldn't take any more of it."

She looked away from us again, out over the alfalfa fields— and a long ways beyond them, at something only she could see. "No roots," she said, "that was part of it, too. No roots.

THE HANGING MAN

Moving here, moving there, always moving—three states and five homesteads in less than ten years. And the fear. And the waiting. This was the last time, I couldn't take it ever again. Not one more minute of his jealousy, his cruelty . . . *his* wickedness."

"Ma'am, you're not making sense—"

"But I am," she said. "Don't you see? He was Jubal Parsons, the Hanging Man."

I started to say something, but she shifted position on the steps just then—and when she did that her face came out of shadow and into the sunlight, and I saw in her eyes a kind of terrible knowledge. It put a chill on my neck like the night wind does when it blows across a graveyard.

"That drifter in Tule River wasn't the first man Jubal hung on account of me," she said. "Not even the first in California. That drifter was the Hanging Man's eighth."

Hero

THE MOB BOILED upstreet from Saloon Row toward the jailhouse. Some of the men in front carried lanterns and torches made out of rag-wrapped sticks soaked in coal oil; Micah could see the flickering light against the black night sky, the wild quivering shadows. But he couldn't see the men themselves, the hooded and masked leaders, from back here where he was at the rear of the pack. He couldn't see Ike Dall neither. Ike Dall was the one who had the hang rope already shaped out into a noose.

Men surged around Micah, yelling, waving arms and clubs and sixguns. He just couldn't keep up on account of his damn game leg. He kept getting jostled, once almost knocked down. Back there at Hardesty's Gambling Hall he'd been right in the thick of it. He'd been the center of attention, by grab. Now they'd forgot all about him and here he was clumping along on his bad leg, not able to see much, getting bumped and pushed with every dragging step. He could feel the excitement, smell the sweat and the heat and the hunger, but he wasn't a part of it no more.

It wasn't right. Hell damn boy, it just wasn't right. Weren't for him, none of this would be happening. Biggest damn thing ever in Cricklewood, Montana, and all on account of him. He was a hero, wasn't he? Back there at Hardesty's, they'd all said so. Back there at Hardesty's, he'd talked and they'd listened to every word—Ike Dall and Lee Wynkoop and Mack Clausen, all of them, everybody who was somebody in and around

HERO

Cricklewood. Stood him right up there next to the bar, bought him drinks, looked at him with respect, and listened to every word he said.

"Micah seen it, didn't you, Micah? What that drifter done?"

"Sure I did. Told Marshal Thrall and I'm tellin' you. Weren't for me, he'd of got clean away."

"You're a hero, Micah. By God you are."

"Well, now. Well, I guess I am."

"Tell it again. Tell us how it was."

"Sure. Sure I will. I seen it all."

"What'd you see?"

"I seen that drifter, that Larrabee, hold up the Wells, Fargo stage. I seen him shoot Tom Porter twice, shoot Tom Porter dead as anybody ever was."

"How'd you come to be out by the Helena road?"

"Mr. Coombs sent me out from the livery, to tell Harv Perkins the singletree on his wagon was fixed a day early. I took the shortcut along the river, like I allus do when I'm headin' down the valley. Forded by Fisherman's Bend and went on through that stand of cottonwoods on the other side. That was where I was, in them trees, when I seen it happen."

"Larrabee had the stage stopped right there, did he?"

"Sure. Right there. Had his sixgun out and he was tellin' Tom to throw down the treasure box."

"And Tom throwed it down?"

"Sure he did. He throwed it right down."

"Never made to use his shotgun or his side gun?"

"No sir. Never made no play at all."

"So Larrabee shot him in cold blood."

"Cold blood—sure! Shot Tom twice. Right off the coach box the first time, then when Tom was lyin' there on the ground, rollin' around with that first bullet in him, Larrabee walked up to him cool as you please and put his sixgun agin Tom's head *and done it to him proper. Blowed Tom's head half off. Blowed it half off and that's a fact."*

"You all heard that. You heard what Micah seen that son of a bitch do to Tom Porter—a decent citizen, a man we all liked and was proud to call friend. I say we don't wait for the circuit judge. What if he lets Larrabee off light? I say we give that murderin' bastard what he deserves here and now, tonight. Now what do you say?"

"Hang him!"

"Stretch his dirty neck!"

"Hang him high!"

Oh, it had been fine back there at Hardesty's. Everybody looking at him the way they done, with respect. Calling him a hero. He'd been somebody then, not just poor crippled-up Micah Hays who done handy work and run errands and shoveled manure down at the Coombs Livery Barn. Oh, it had been fine! But now—now they'd forgot him again, left him behind, left him out of what was going to happen on *his* account. They were all moving upstreet to the jailhouse with their lanterns and their torches and their hunger, leaving him practically alone where he couldn't do or see a damn thing . . .

Micah stopped trying to run on his game leg and limped along slow, watching the mob, wanting to be a part of it but wanting more to see everything that happened after the mob got to the jailhouse. Then he thought: Why, I *can* see it all! Sure I can! I know just where I got to go.

He hobbled ahead to the alley alongside Burley's Feed and Grain, went down it to the staircase built up the side wall. The stairs led to a railed gallery overlooking the street, and to the offices of the town lawyer, Mr. Spivey, that had been built on top of the feed-store roof. Micah stumped up the stairs and went past the dark offices and on down to the far end of the gallery.

Hell damn boy! He sure *could* see from up here, clear as anybody could want. The mob was close to the jailhouse now; in the dancy light from the lanterns and torches, he could make out the hooded shape of Ike Dall with his hang-rope noose held high, the shapes of Lee Wynkoop and Mack Clausen and the others who were leading the pack. He could see that big old shade cottonwood off to one side of the jail, too, with its one gnarly limb that stretched out over the street. That was where they was going to hang the drifter. Ike Dall had said so, back there at Hardesty's. *"We don't have to take him far, by Christ. We'll string him up right there next to the jail."*

The front door of the jailhouse opened and out come Marshal Thrall and his deputy, Ben Dietrich. Micah leaned out over the railing, squinting, feeling the excitement scurry up and down inside his chest like a mouse on a wall. Marshal Thrall had a shotgun in his hands and Ben Dietrich held a rifle. The marshal commenced to yelling, but whatever it was got lost in the noise from the mob. Mob didn't slow down none, neither, when old Thrall started waving that Greener of his. Marshal wasn't going to shoot nobody, Ike Dall had said. *"Why, we're all Thrall's friends and neighbors. Ben Dietrich's, too. They ain't goin' to shoot up their friends and neighbors, are they? Just to stop the lynching of a murderin' son of a bitch like Larrabee?"*

No sir, they sure wasn't. That mob didn't slow down none at all. It surged right ahead, right on around Marshal Thrall and Ben Dietrich like floodwaters around a sandbar, and swallowed them both up and carried them right on into the jailhouse.

A hell of a racket come from inside. Pretty soon the pack parted down the middle and Micah could see four or five men carrying that drifter up in the air, hands tied behind him, the same way you'd carry a side of butchered beef. Hell damn boy! Everybody was whooping it up, waving torches and lanterns and twirling light around in the dark like a bunch of kids with pinwheel sparklers. It put Micah in mind of an Independence Day celebration. By grab, that was just what it was like. Fireworks on the Fourth of July.

Well, they carried that murdering Larrabee on over to the shade cottonwood. He was screaming things, that drifter was—screaming the whole way. Micah couldn't hear most of it above the crowd noise, but he caught a few of the words. And one whole sentence: "I tell you, I didn't do it!"

"Why, sure you did," Micah said out loud. "Sure you did. I seen you do it, didn't I?"

Ike Dall throwed his rope over the cottonwood's gnarly limb, caught the other end and give it to somebody, and then he put that noose around Larrabee's neck and drew it tight. Somebody else brung a saddle horse around, held him steady whilst they hoisted the drifter onto his back. That Larrabee was screaming like a woman now.

Micah leaned hard against the gallery railing. His mouth was dry, real dry; he couldn't even work up no spit to wet it. He'd never seen a lynching before. There'd been plenty in Montana Territory—more'n a dozen over in Beaverhead and Madison counties a few years back, when the vigilantes done for Henry Plummer and his gang of desperadoes—but never one in Cricklewood nor any of the other towns Micah had lived in.

The drifter screamed and screamed. Then Micah saw everybody back off some, away from the horse Larrabee was on, and Ike Dall raised his arm and brought it down smack on the cayuse's rump. Horse jumped ahead, frog-stepping. And Larrabee quit screaming and commenced to dancing in the air all loosey-goosey, like a puppet on the end of a string. Before long, though, the dancing slowed down and then it quit altogether. That's done him, Micah thought. And everybody in the mob knew it, too, because they all backed off some more and stood there in a half-circle, staring up at the drifter hanging still and straight in the smoky light.

Micah stared too. He leaned against the railing and stared and stared, and kept on staring long after the mob started to break up.

Hell damn boy, he thought over and over. Hell damn boy, if that sure wasn't something to see!

It took the best part of a week for the town to get back to normal. There was plenty more excitement during that week—county law coming in, representatives from the territorial governor's office in Helena, newspaper people, all kinds of curious strangers. For Micah it was kind of like the lynching went on and on, a week-long celebration like none other he'd ever been part of. Folks kept asking him questions, interviewing him for newspapers, buying him drinks, shaking his hand and clapping his back and calling him a hero the way the men had done that night at Hardesty's. Oh, it was fine. It was almost as fine as when he'd been the center of attention before the lynch mob got started.

But then it all come to an end. The law and the newspaper people and the strangers went away; Cricklewood settled down to what it had been before the big event, and Micah settled back into his humdrum job at the Coombs Livery Barn and his nights on the straw bunk in one corner of the loft. He did his handy work, ran errands, shoveled manure—and the townsfolk and ranchers and cowhands stopped buying him drinks, stopped shaking his hand and clapping his back and calling him hero, stopped paying much attention to him at all. It was the same as before, like he was nobody, like he didn't hardly even exist. Mack Clausen snubbed him on the street no more than two weeks after the lynching. The one time he tried to get Ike Dall to talk with him about that night, how it had felt putting the noose around Larrabee's neck, Ike wouldn't have none of it. Why, Ike claimed he hadn't even been there that night, hadn't been part of the mob—said that lie right to Micah's face!

Four weeks passed. Five. Micah did his handy work and ran errands and shoveled manure and now nobody even *mentioned* that night no more, not to him and not to each other. Like it never happened. Like they was ashamed of it or something.

Micah was feeling low the hot Saturday morning he come down the loft ladder and started toward the harness room like he always done first thing. But this wasn't like other mornings because a man was curled up sleeping in one of the stalls near the back doors. Big man, whiskers on his face, dust on his trail clothes. Micah had never seen him before.

Mr. Coombs was up at the other end of the barn, forking hay for the two roan saddle horses he kept for rent. Micah went on up there and said, "Morning, Mr. Coombs."

"Well, Micah. Down late again, eh?"

". . . I reckon so."

"Getting to be a habit lately," Mr. Coombs said. "I don't like it, Micah. See that you start coming down on time from now on, hear?"

"Yes, sir. Mr. Coombs, who's that sleepin' in the back stall?"

"Just some drifter. He didn't say his name."

"Drifter?"

"Came in half-drunk last night, paid me four bits to let him sleep in here. Not the first time I've rented out a stall to a human animal and it won't be the last."

Mr. Coombs turned and started forking some more hay. Micah went away toward the harness room, then stopped after ten paces and stood quiet for a space. And then, moving slow, he hobbled over to where the fire ax hung and pulled it down and limped back behind Mr. Coombs and swung the axe up and shut his eyes and swung the ax down. When he opened his eyes again Mr. Coombs was lying there with the back of his head cleaved open and blood and brains spilled out like pulp out of a split melon.

Hell damn boy, Micah thought.

Then he dropped the ax and run to the front doors and threw them open and run out onto Main Street yelling at the top of his voice, "Murder! It's murder! Some damn drifter killed Mr. Coombs! Split his head wide open with a fire ax. I seen him do it, I seen it, I seen the whole thing!"

McIntosh's Chute

It was right after supper and we were all settled around the cookfire, smoking, none of us saying much because it was well along in the roundup and we were all dog-tired from the long days of riding and chousing cows out of brush-clogged coulees. I wasn't doing anything except taking in the night—warm Montana fall night, sky all hazed with stars, no moon to speak of. Then, of a sudden, something come streaking across all that velvet-black and silver from east to west: a ball of smoky red-orange with a long fiery tail. Everybody stirred around and commenced to gawping and pointing. But not for long. Quick as it had come, the thing was gone beyond the broken sawteeth of the Rockies.

There was a hush. Then young Poley said, "What in hell was *that*?" He was just eighteen and big for his britches in more ways than one. But that heavenly fireball had taken him down to an awed whisper.

"Comet," Cass Buckram said.

"That fire-tail . . . whooee!" Poley said. "I never seen nothing like it. Comet, eh? Well, it's the damnedest sight a man ever set eyes on."

"Damnedest sight a *button* ever set eyes on, maybe."

"I ain't a button!"

"You are from where I sit," Cass said. "Big shiny man-sized button with your threads still dangling."

Everybody laughed except Poley. Being as he was the youngest on the roundup crew, he'd taken his share of ragging since we'd left the Box 8 and he was about fed up with it. He said, "Well, what do *you* know about it, oldtimer?"

That didn't faze Cass. He was close to sixty, though you'd never know it to look at him or watch him when he worked cattle or at anything else, but age didn't mean much to him. He was of a philosophical turn of mind. You were what you were and no sense in pretending otherwise—that was how he looked at it.

In his younger days he'd been an adventuresome gent. Worked at jobs most of us wouldn't have tried in places we'd never even hoped to visit. Oil rigger in Texas and Oklahoma, logger in Oregon, fur trapper in the Canadian Barrens, prospector in the Yukon during the '98 Rush, cowhand in half a dozen states and territories. He'd packed more living into the past forty-odd years than a whole regiment of men, and he didn't mind talking about his experiences. No, he sure didn't mind. First time I met him, I'd taken him for a blowhard. Plenty took him that way in the beginning, on account of his windy nature. But the stories he told were true, or at least every one had a core of truth in it. He had too many facts and a whole warbag full of mementoes and photographs and such to back 'em up.

All you had to do was prime him a little—and without knowing it, young Poley had primed him just now. But that was all right with the rest of us. Cass had honed his storytelling skills over the years; one of his yarns was always worthwhile entertainment.

He said to the kid, "I saw more strange things before I was twenty than you'll ever see."

"Cowflop."

"Correct word is bullshit," Cass said, solemn, and everybody laughed again. "But neither one is accurate."

"I suppose you seen something stranger and more spectacular than that there comet."

"Twice as strange and three times as spectacular."
"Cowflop."
"Fact. Ninth wonder of the world, in its way."
"Well? What was it?"
"McIntosh and his chute."
"Chute? What chute? Who was McIntosh?"
"Keep your lip buttoned, button, and I'll tell you. I'll tell you about *the* damnedest sight I or any other man ever laid eyes on."

Happened more than twenty years ago [Cass went on], in southern Oregon in the early nineties. I'd had my fill of fur-trapping in the Barrens and developed a hankering to see what timber work was like, so I'd come on down into Oregon and hooked on with a logging outfit near Coos Bay. But for the first six months I was just a bullcook, not a timberjack. Low-down work, bullcooking—cleaning up after the jacks, making up their bunks, cutting firewood, helping out in the kitchen. Without experience, that's the only kind of job you can get in a decent logging camp. Boss finally put me on one of the yarding crews, but even then there was no thrill in the work and the wages were low. So I was ready for a change of venue when word filtered in that a man named Saginaw Tom McIntosh was hiring for his camp on Black Mountain.

McIntosh was from Michigan and had made a pile logging in the North Woods. What had brought him west to Oregon was the opportunity to buy better than 25,000 acres of virgin timberland on Black Mountain. He'd rebuilt an old dam on the Klamath River nearby that had been washed out by high water, built a sawmill and a millpond below the dam, and then started a settlement there that he named after himself. And once he had a camp operating on the mountain, first thing he did was construct a chute, or skidway, down to the river.

Word of McIntosh's chute spread just as fast and far as word that he was hiring timber beasts at princely wages. It was supposed to be an engineering marvel, unlike any other logging chute ever built. Some scoffed when they were told about it; claimed it was just one of those tall stories that get flung around among Northwest loggers, like the one about Paul Bunyan and Babe the blue ox. Me, I was willing to give Saginaw Tom McIntosh the benefit of the doubt. I figured that if he was half the man he was talked of being, he could accomplish just about anything he set his mind to.

He had two kinds of reputation. First, as a demon logger—a man who could get timber cut faster and turned into board lumber quicker than any other boss jack. And second, as a ruthless cold-hearted son of a bitch who bullied his men, worked them like animals, and wasn't above using fists, peaveys, calks, and any other handy weapon if the need arose. Rumor had it that he—

What's that, boy? No, I ain't going to say any more about that chute just yet. I'll get to it in good time. You just keep your pants on and let me tell this my own way.

Well, rumor had it that McIntosh was offering top dollar because it was the only way he could get jacks to work steady for him. That and his reputation didn't bother me one way or another. I'd dealt with hardcases before, and have since. So I determined to see what Saginaw Tom and his chute and Black Mountain were all about.

I quit the Coos Bay outfit and traveled down to McIntosh's settlement on the Klamath. Turned out to be bigger than I'd expected. The sawmill was twice the size of the one up at Coos Bay, and there was a blacksmith shop, a box factory, a hotel and half a dozen boardinghouses, two big stores, a school, two churches, and a lodge hall. McIntosh may have been a son of a bitch, but he sure did know how to get maximum production and how to provide for his men and their families.

I hired on at the mill, and the next day a crew chief named

MCINTOSH'S CHUTE

Lars Nilson drove me and another new man, a youngster called Johnny Cline, upriver to the Black Mountain camp. Long, hot trip in the back of a buckboard, up steep grades and past gold-mining claims strung along the rough-water river. Nilson told us there was bad blood between McIntosh and those miners. They got gold out of the sand by trapping silt in wing dams, and they didn't like it when McIntosh's river drivers built holding cribs along the banks or herded long chains of logs downstream to the cribs and then on to the mill. There hadn't been any trouble yet, but it could erupt at any time; feelings were running high on both sides.

Heat and flies and hornets deviled us all the way up into scrub timber: lodgepole, jack, and yellow pine. The bigger trees—white sugar pine—grew higher up, and what fine old trees they were. Clean-growing, hardly any underbrush. Huge trunks that rose up straight from brace roots close to four feet broad, and no branches on 'em until thirty to forty feet above the ground. Every lumberman's dream, the cut-log timber on that mountain.

McIntosh was taking full advantage of it, too. His camp was twice the size of most—two enormous bunkhouses, a cook-shack, a barn and blacksmith shop, clusters of sheds and shanties and heavy wagons, corrals full of work horses and oxen. Close to a hundred men, altogether. And better than two dozen big wheels, stinger-tongue and slip-tongue both—

What's a big wheel? Just that, boy—wheels ten and twelve feet high, some made of wood and some of iron, each pair connected by an axle that had a chain and a long tongue poking back from the middle. Four-horse team drew each one. Man on the wheel crew dug a shallow trench under one or two logs, depending on their size; loader pushed the chain through it under the logs and secured it to the axle; driver lunged his team ahead and the tongue slid forward and yanked on the chain to lift the front end of the logs off the ground. Harder the horses pulled, the higher the logs hung. When the team came to a stop, the logs dropped and dragged. Only trouble was, sometimes they didn't drop and drag just right—didn't act as a brake like they were supposed to—and the wheel horses got their hind legs smashed. Much safer and faster to use a steam lokey to get cut logs out of the woods, but laying narrow gauge track takes time and so does ordering a lokey and having it packed in sections up the side of a wilderness mountain. McIntosh figured to have his track laid and a lokey operating by the following spring. Meanwhile, it was the big wheels and the teams of horses and oxen and men that had to do the heavy work.

Now then. The chute—McIntosh's chute.

First I seen of it was across the breadth of the camp, at the edge of a steep drop-off: the chute head, a big two-level platform built of logs. Cut logs were stacked on the top level as they came off the big wheels, by jacks crowhopping over the deck with cant hooks. On the lower level other jacks looped a cable around the foremost log, and a donkey engine wound up the cable and hauled the log forward into a trough built at the outer edge of the platform. You follow me so far?

Well, that was all I could see until Nilson took Johnny Cline and me over close to the chute head. From the edge of the drop-off you had a miles-wide view—long snaky stretches of the Klamath, timberland all the way south to the California border. But it wasn't the vista that had my attention; it was the chute itself. An engineering marvel, all right, that near took my breath away.

McIntosh and his crew had cut a channel in the rocky hillside straight on down to the river bank, and lined the sides and bottom with flat-hewn logs—big ones at the sides and smaller ones on the bottom, all worn glass-smooth. Midway along was a kind of trestle that spanned an outcrop and acted as a speed-brake. Nothing legendary about that chute: it was the longest built up to that time, maybe the longest ever. More than twenty-six hundred feet of timber had gone into the construction, top to bottom.

While I was gawking down at it, somebody shouted, "Clear back!" and right away Nilson herded Johnny Cline and me onto a hummock to one side. At the chute head a chain of logs was lined and ready, held back by an iron bar wedged into the rock. Far down below one of the river crew showed a white flag, and as soon as he did the chute tender yanked the iron bar aside and the first log shuddered through and down.

After a hundred feet or so, it began to pick up speed. You could hear it squealing against the sides and bottom of the trough. By the time it went over the trestle and into the lower part of the chute, it was a blur. Took just eighteen seconds for it to drop more than eight hundred feet to the river, and when it hit the splash was bigger than a barn and the fan of water drenched trees on both banks—

"Hell!" young Poley interrupted. "I don't believe none of that. You're funning us, Cass."

"Be damned if I am. What don't you believe?"

"None of it. Chute twenty-six hundred feet long, logs shooting down over eight hundred feet in less than twenty seconds, splashes bigger than a barn . . ."

"Well, it's the gospel truth. So's the rest of it. Sides and bottom a third of the way down were burned black from the friction—black as coal. On cold mornings you could see smoke from the logs going down: that's how fast they traveled. Went even faster when there was frost, so the river crew had to drive spikes in the chute's bottom end to slow 'em up. Even so, sometimes a log would hit the river with enough force to split it in half, clean, like it'd gone through a buzz saw. But I expect you don't believe none of that, either."

Poley grunted. "Not hardly."

MCINTOSH'S CHUTE

I said, "Well, *I* believe it, Cass. Man can do just about anything he sets his mind to, like you said, if he wants it bad enough. That chute must of been something. I can sure see why it was the damnedest thing you ever saw."

"No, it wasn't," Cass said.

"What? But you said—"

"No, I didn't. McIntosh's chute was a wonder but not the damnedest thing I ever saw."

"Then what *is*?" Poley demanded.

"If I wasn't interrupted every few minutes, you'd of found out by now." Cass glared at him. "You going to be quiet and let me get to it or you intend to keep flapping your gums so this here story takes all night?"

Poley wasn't cowed, but he did button his lip. And surprised us all—maybe even himself—by keeping it buttoned for the time being.

I thought I might get put on one of the wheel crews [Cass resumed], but I'd made the mistake of telling Nilson I'd worked a yarding crew up at Coos Bay, so a yarding crew was where I got put on Black Mountain. Working as a choke-setter in the slash out back of the camp—man that sets heavy cable chokers around the end of a log that's fallen down a hillside or into a ravine so the log can be hauled out by means of a donkey engine. Hard, sweaty, dangerous work in the best of camps, and McIntosh's was anything but the best. The rumors had been right about that, too. We worked long hours for our pay, seven days a week. And if a man dropped from sheer exhaustion, he was expected to get up under his own power—and was docked for the time he spent lying down.

Johnny Cline got put on the same crew, as a whistle-punk on the donkey, and him and me took up friendly. He was a Californian, from down near San Francisco; young and feisty and too smart-ass for his own good . . . some like you, Poley.

But decent enough, underneath. His brother was a logger somewhere in Canada, and he'd determined to try his hand too. He was about as green as me, but you could see that logging was in his blood in a way that it wasn't in mine. I knew I'd be moving on to other things one day; he knew he'd be a logger till the day he died.

I got along with Nilson and most of the other timber beasts, but Saginaw Tom McIntosh was another matter. If anything, he was worse than his reputation—mean clear through, with about as much decency as a vulture on a fence post waiting for something to die. Giant of a man, face weathered the color of heartwood, droopy yellow mustache stained with juice from the quids of Spearhead tobacco he always kept stowed in one cheek, eyes like pale fire that gave you the feeling you'd been burned whenever they touched you. Stalked around camp in worn cruisers, stagged corduroy pants, and steel-calked boots, yelling out orders, knocking men down with his fists if they didn't ask how high when he hollered jump. Ran that camp the way a hardass warden runs a prison. Everybody hated him, including me and Johnny Cline before long. But most of the jacks feared him, too, which was how he kept them in line.

He drove all his crews hard, demanding that a dozen turns of logs go down his chute every day to feed the saws working twenty-four hours at the mill. Cut lumber was fetching more than a hundred dollars per thousand feet at the time and he wanted to keep production at a fever pitch before the heavy winter rains set in. There was plenty of grumbling among the men, and tempers were short, but nobody quit the camp. Pay was too good, even with all the abuse that went along with it.

I'd been at the Back Mountain camp three weeks when the real trouble started. One of the gold miners down on the Klamath, man named Coogan, got drunk and decided to tear up a holding crib because he blamed McIntosh for ruining his claim. McIntosh flew into a rage when he heard about it. He ranted and raved for half a day about how he'd had enough of those goddamn miners. Then, when he'd worked himself up enough, he ordered a dozen jacks down on a night raid to bust up Coogan's wing dam and raise some hell with the other miners' claims. The jacks didn't want to do it but he bullied them into it with threats and promises of bonus money.

But the miners were expecting retaliation; had joined forces and were waiting when the jacks showed up. There was a riverbank brawl, mostly with fists and ax handles, but with a few shots fired too. Three timber stiffs were hurt bad enough so that they had to be carried back to camp and would be laid up for a while.

The county law came next day and threatened to close McIntosh down if there was any more trouble. That threw him into another fit. Kind of man he was, he took it out on the men in the raiding party.

"What kind of jack lets a gold-grubber beat him down?" he yelled at them. "You buggers ain't worth the name timberjack. If I didn't need your hands and backs, I'd send the lot of you packing. As is, I'm cutting your pay. And you three that can't work—you get no pay at all until you can hoist your peaveys and swing your axes."

One of the jacks challenged him. McIntosh kicked the man in the crotch, knocked him down, and then gave him a case of logger's smallpox: pinned his right arm to the ground with those steel calks of his. There were no other challenges. But in all those bearded faces you could see the hate that was building for McIntosh. You could feel it too; it was in the air, crackles of it like electricity in a storm.

Another week went by. There was no more trouble with the miners, but McIntosh drove his crews with a vengeance. Up to fifteen turns of logs down the chute each day. The big-wheel crews hauling until their horses were ready to drop; and two did drop dead in harness, while another two had to be destroyed when logs crushed their hind legs on the drag. Buckers and fallers working the slash from dawn to dark, so that the skirl of crosscuts and bucksaws and the thud of axes rolled like constant thunder across the face of Black Mountain.

Some men can stand that kind of killing pace without busting down one way or another, and some men can't. Johnny Cline was one of those who couldn't. He was hot-headed, like I said before, and ten times every day and twenty times every night he cursed McIntosh and damned his black soul. Then, one day when he'd had all he could swallow, he made the mistake of cursing and damning McIntosh to the boss logger's face.

The yarding crew we were on was deep in the slash, struggling to get logs out of a small valley. It was coming on dusk and we'd been at it for hours; we were all bone-tired. I set the choker around the end of yet another log, and the hook-tender signaled Johnny Cline, who stood behind him with one hand on the wire running to the whistle on the donkey engine. When Johnny pulled the wire and the short blast sounded, the cable snapped tight and the big log started to move, its nose plowing up dirt and crushing saplings in its path. But as it came up the slope it struck a sunken log, as sometimes happens, and shied off. The hook-tender signaled for slack, but Johnny didn't give it fast enough to keep the log from burying its nose in the roots of a fir stump.

McIntosh saw it. He'd come catfooting up and was ten feet from the donkey engine. He ran up to Johnny yelling, "You stupid goddamn greenhorn!" and gave him a shove that knocked the kid halfway down to where the log was stumped.

Johnny caught himself and scrambled back up the incline. I could see the hate afire in his eyes and I tried to get between him and McIntosh, but he brushed me aside. He put his face up close to the boss logger's, spat out a string of cuss words, and finished up with, "I've had all I'm gonna take from you, you son of a bitch." And then he swung with his right hand.

But all he hit was air. McIntosh had seen it coming; he stepped inside the punch and spat tobacco juice into Johnny's face. The squirt and spatter threw the kid off balance and blinded him at the same time—left him wide open for McIntosh to wade in with fists and knees.

McIntosh seemed to go berserk, as if all the rage and meanness had built to an explosion point inside him and Johnny's words had triggered it. Johnny Cline never had a chance. McIntosh beat him to the ground, kept on beating him even though me and some of the others fought to pull him off. And when he saw his chance he raised up one leg and he stomped the kid's face with his calks—drove those sharp steel spikes down into Johnny's face as if he was grinding a bug under his heel.

Johnny screamed once, went stiff, then lay still. Nilson and some others had come running up by then and it took six of us to drag McIntosh away before he could smallpox Johnny Cline a second time. He battled us for a few seconds, like a crazy man; then, all at once, the wildness went out of him. But he was no more human when it did. He tore himself loose, and without a word, without any concern for the boy he'd stomped, he stalked off through the slash.

Johnny Cline's face was a red ruin, pitted and torn by half a hundred steel points. I thought he was dead at first, but when I got down beside him I found a weak pulse. Four of us picked him up and carried him to our bunkhouse.

The bullcook and me cleaned the blood off him and doctored his wounds as best we could. But he was in a bad way. His right eye was gone, pierced by one of McIntosh's calks, and he was hurt inside, too, for he kept coughing up red foam. There just wasn't much we could do for him. The nearest doctor was thirty miles away; by the time somebody went and fetched him back, it would be too late. I reckon we all knew from the first that Johnny Cline would be dead by morning.

There was no more work for any of us that day. None of the jacks in our bunkhouse took any grub, either, nor slept much as the night wore on. We all just sat around in little groups with our lamps lit, talking low, smoking and drinking coffee or tea. Checking on Johnny now and then. Waiting.

He never regained consciousness. An hour before dawn the bullcook went to look at him and announced, "He's gone." The waiting was done. Yes, and so were Saginaw Tom McIntosh and the Black Mountain camp.

Nilson and the other crew chiefs had a meeting outside, between the two bunkhouses. The rest of us kept our places. When Nilson and the two others who bunked in our building came back in, it was plain enough from their expressions what had been decided. And plainer still when the three of them shouldered their peaveys. Loggers will take so much from a boss like Saginaw Tom McIntosh—only so much and no more. What he'd done to Johnny Cline was the next to last straw; Johnny dying was the final one.

At the door Nilson said, "We're on our way to cut down a rotted tree. Rest of you can stay or join us, as you see fit. But you'll all keep your mouths shut either way. Clear?"

Nobody had any objections. Nilson turned and went out with the other two chiefs.

Well, none of the men in our bunkhouse stayed, nor did anybody in the other one. We were all of the same mind. I thought I knew what would happen to McIntosh, but I was wrong. The crew heads weren't fixing to give him the same as he gave Johnny Cline. No, they had other plans. When a logging crew turns, it turns hard—and it gives no quarter.

The near-dawn dark was chill and damp, and I don't mind saying it put a shiver on my back. We all walked quiet through it to McIntosh's shanty—close to a hundred of us, so he heard us coming anyway. But not in time to get up a weapon. He fought with the same wildness he had earlier but he didn't have any more chance than he gave Johnny Cline. Nilson stunned him with his peavey. Then half a dozen men stuffed him into his clothes and his blood-stained boots and took him out.

Straight across the camp we went, with four of the crew heads carrying McIntosh by the arms and legs. He came around just before they got him to the edge of the drop-off. He realized what was going to happen to him, looked like, at about the same time I did.

He was struggling fierce, bellowing curses, when Nilson and the others pitched him into the chute.

He went down slow at first, the way one of the big logs always did. Clawing at the flat-hewn sides, trying to dig his calks into the glass-smooth bottom logs. Then he commenced to pick up speed, and his yells turned to banshee screams. Two hundred feet down the screaming stopped; he was just a blur by then. His clothes started to smoke from the friction, then burst into flame. When he went sailing over the trestle he was a lump of fire that lit up the dark . . . then a streak of fire as he shot down into the lower section . . . then a fireball with a tail longer and brighter than the one on that comet a while ago, so bright the river and the woods on both banks showed plain as day for two or three seconds before he smacked the river—smacked it and went out in a splash and steamy sizzle you could see and hear all the way up at the chute head.

"And that," Cass Buckram finished, "*that*, by God, was the damnedest sight I or any other man ever set eyes on—McIntosh going down McIntosh's chute, eight hundred feet straight into hell."

None of us argued with him. Not even Poley the button.

Fyfe and the Drummers

O<small>LD-TIME DRUMMERS</small> was a peculiar bunch.

It's a fact. I been tending bar here for near forty years—F.X. Fyfe, at your service—and I seen all sorts of folks come through New Appia and the New Appia Hotel, good and bad and some strange. But drummers back before the century turned . . . well, there just weren't none like them peckerwoods. Whiskey drummers, cigar drummers, medicine drummers, hardware drummers, dry-goods drummers, lightning-rod drummers, windmill drummers . . . they was *all* a caution.

You take their general appearance. Not one of them salesmen ever set out to dress like other folks. No sir. They all wore fancy suits that might of been made out of horse blankets, they was that flashy. And waistcoats in different colors than the suits, some decorated with flower patterns that set you in mind of window drapery. And stiff shirts and four-in-hand ties and stickpins with big fake jewels in 'em. And patent-leather shoes shined bright enough so's you could shave and comb your hair looking into the gloss. Most of 'em wore waxed moustaches, too, sometimes dyed pure black, with the ends so stiff and pointy you could've used one to pick your teeth.

Then there was what come out when them boys opened their mouths. Talk? Lordy, old-time drummers could talk a miser out of his gold, a girl out of her drawers, and a politician out of three bought votes. Charm by the carload, that's what they had, and weren't none of it any deeper than a skin of ice after

FYFE AND THE DRUMMERS

the first hard freeze. Them peckerwoods didn't have to *work* at being salesmen; they was just natural-born liars and flimflammers.

You think cowboys is hard drinkers? Why, they're pikers compared to drummers. More times than I can count I threw one out, put another to bed, and served 'em Fyfe's Own Hangover Cure on the morning after. You think Frenchmen is great lovers? I never seen a drummer that wasn't hell-on-wheels with the ladies—or thought he was, or pretended he was. You think minstrel-show and vaudeville comedians know a passel of comical stories? Why, drummers could tell stories for a week straight and never run out. Most of their jokes was bawdy, some was even funny, and danged if they couldn't make you laugh now and then at one that *wasn't* funny.

Yes sir, all them old-timers was a caution. But I reckon the patent medicine peddlers was the most cockeyed of the lot. How so? Well, I'll give you a first-class example.

This here happened back in the early Nineties. Late January, it was. Cold, raw night, mostly wind with a little sleet in it. Wasn't many guests registered at the hotel—never is, that time of year—and there was only half a dozen or so steady customers in the bar parlor when Charley Tuggle walked in.

Charley Tuggle had been a patent medicine drummer for half his forty years—to hear him tell it, anyhow. I knew him tolerable well on account of he'd been coming through New Appia twice a year for the previous seven, always stopped here at the hotel, and always come into the bar parlor to drink hot whiskey with sugar water and chew my ear. He wore loud checked suits and fancy flannel waistcoats—I recollect the one on this night was tan, with orange nasturtiums embroidered on it—and he had muttonchop whispers to go with his pointy moustache. He talked faster than most drummers, which is some fast, and told better dirty stories, too.

Now Tuggle sold all sorts of drugs and medicines—every-

– 140 –

thing from hair tonic to laxatives, from Turkish Pile Ointment to Lydia Pinkham's Vegetable Compound for Ladies. But what he sold best of all was a snake-oil product called Cherokee's Magical Herb Bitters. Likely most medicine drummers never touched a drop of what they peddled, but Tuggle swore up and down that he drank a full bottle of Cherokee's Magical Herb Bitters every week. I believed him, too, as passionate as he was on the subject. He was in the peak of health and says he owed it all to them bitters. Says it to anybody who'd listen. Says it to me every time he bellied up to my bar.

He come in after supper, this night I'm telling about. Carrying a tolerable load (which was nothing unusual), on account of he'd been imbibing spirits most of the day with his best customer, Chet Iams over to the drugstore. He ordered a hot whiskey with sugar water, made some small talk about the weather, and then commenced to bending my ear about them magical bitters of his. Not talking soft, neither. The other patrons sidled off, lest he include them in his pitch, but there wasn't nowhere for me to go. So I listened same as if I'd never heard it all before. Part of my job is to listen, even if it ain't always the best part.

Tuggle started out by saying that Cherokee's Magical Herb Bitters was just the tonic a man needed to stay fit in inclement weather like we was having, for it was the greatest blood and nerve medicine ever manufactured by human beings. Then he says, "Mr. Fyfe, this miracle tonic cures all bilious derangements and drives out the foul corruption that contaminates the blood and causes decay. It stimulates and enlivens the vital functions, being as it is a pure vegetable compound and free from all mineral poisons. It promotes energy and strength, restores and preserves health, and infuses new life and vigor throughout the entire system." And so on and so forth.

He was just getting warmed up, old Tuggle was, when this young whippersnapper named Peckham come waltzing in.

Now Peckham was also a patent medicine drummer—a newcomer to our fair town, one of them freelancers that work for different manufacturers and don't have a set territory. Full of piss and vinegar, was young Peckham. Full of corn whiskey, too, this night, on account of bending elbows all day long with a customer *he* was trying to impress. Weren't usual for two snake-oil peddlers to come through town at the same time, and this Peckham was new on the road, so him and Tuggle wasn't acquainted. Not yet, they wasn't.

Well, here come Peckham into the bar parlor, weaving some and toting his sample case, just as Tuggle declaims that Cherokee's Magical Herb Bitters is the purest, safest, and most effectual medicine known to mankind, and that there ain't no sore it won't heal, no pain it won't subdue, and no disease it won't cure.

Peckham stopped dead in his tracks, listening to this with a scowl. Then he twisted one of his sandy moustaches, and when Tuggle paused to draw a breath, he says loud and clear, "Bunkum."

That got everybody's attention, including Tuggle's. Old Charley come around, looked the youngster up and down with one squinty eye, and asks him soft and chilly to repeat himself.

"Bunkum," Peckham says again, just as loud. "Pure bunkum."

"Is that so, my brash young fellow?" Tuggle says. "And just what do you know about such matters?"

"Everything I need to know," Peckham counters. "Why, whatever puny concoction you're hawking can't hold a candle to Dr. Wallmann's Celebrated Nerve and Brain Tonic."

"Dr. Wallmann's what?" Tuggle says, haughty. "I have never heard of it."

"You will," the boy says. "You surely will. It is brand

spanking new—the finest, purest blood, nerve, and brain medicine ever made for the benefit of mankind. Bar none."

"Bunkum," Tuggle says.

Well, it got Sunday-sermon quiet in there. The two of 'em looked each other over like a couple of fancy fighting cocks. Then Peckham strutted up to the bar, opened his sample case, took out a brown bottle of this Dr. Wallmann's Celebrated Nerve and Brain Tonic, and smacked it down with a flourish. "Behold," he says. "The new wonder oil—the discovery of the ages."

Tuggle didn't even glance at the bottle. He reached inside his loud checked coat, produced a brown bottle of Cherokee's Magical Herb Bitters, and smacked that down with an even grander flourish. "Behold," he says. "The old wonder oil—the *true* discovery of the ages."

The pair of 'em glared at each other. Then Peckham says by way of a challenge, "Dr. Wallmann's Celebrated Nerve and Brain Tonic cures any affliction you can name, and more afflictions and derangements than any other product on the face of the globe."

"Oh it does, does it?" Tuggle says. "Womb complaints and uterine affections, mayhap?"

"Of course."

"Formation of gas in the bowels?"

"Naturally."

"Sciatica and neuralgia?"

"Most assuredly."

"Chronic rheumatism, pleurisy, gout?"

"With ease, sir. With ease."

"Well, so does Cherokee's Magical Herb Bitters," Tuggle says like a senator to a rube, "and with even *greater* ease. My wonder bitters also cures dyspepsia, costiveness, bad breath, palpitations of the heart, the old Sunday sick headache, persistent and obstinate constipation, fever and ague, and salt rheum."

"So does my celebrated tonic," Peckham says. "Not to mention eczema, erysipelas, tetter, cankers, and water brash."

"But not ulcerated kidneys," Tuggle says.

"Ulcerated kidneys *and* inflamed kidneys."

"Highly colored urine?"

"*And* greasy froth in the urine."

"Asthma, bronchitis, epilepsy?"

"*And* purulent ulcers, scrofula, and deafness."

By this time Tuggle was red in the face—so red I couldn't help but wonder if Cherokee's Magical Herb Bitters also cured apoplexy. He all but shouts at the young upstart, "Belching of wind and food after eating?"

"With only two teaspoons."

"Lusterless eyeballs?"

"Three tablespoons."

"Catarrh of the bladder?"

"Half a bottle, no more."

"Lost manhood?"

"Guaranteed after the ingestion of but a single bottle."

"Liar!" Tuggle yells. "Charlatan! Only Cherokee's Magical Herb Bitters can stiffen a flaccid man's resolve!"

That got the boy's back up. He moved close to Tuggle and says right in his face, "How dare you call me a liar? I demand an apology, sir."

"To hell with your apology," Tuggle says. "And to hell with Dr. Pipsqueak's Celebrated Nerve and Brain Tonic!"

"Oh yes?" Peckham says, sparking some himself. "Well, to hell with Quack's Magical damned Bitters!"

I leaned over the bar along in here and says, "Now gents, settle down, let's keep matters peaceable," but neither of 'em paid me any mind. They was nose to nose, glaring and growling.

"Diarrhea!"
"Lumbago!"
"Weak lungs!"
"Milk leg!"
"Chilblains and bunions!"
"Distressing heat flashes!"
"Diseased glands!"
"Carbuncles and cutaneous eruptions!"
"Dandruff and falling of the hair!"
"Pressure on top of the head!"

"I'll give *you* pressure on top of the head!" Tuggle roars, and danged if he don't fetch young Peckham a hellacious thump smack on the cranium.

Well, the blow knocked Peckham to his knees, but not for long. The youngster bounced back up like a jack-in-the-box, bellowing and snarling, and give old Charley a jolt over the heart. Next thing I knew, the two of 'em was mixing it up like a couple of crapulous prize-fighters at the county fair—all flailing arms and patent-leather shoes and cuss words, some of which even I was amazed to hear.

By the time I got my bungstarter and come over the bar, they was down on the floor, rolling around and punching, gouging and kicking each other. Everybody else had scattered out of harm's way. I leaned in and give Peckham a clout on the shoulder with the bungstarter, on account of he'd picked up a spittoon and was aiming to brain Tuggle with it. Wasn't my best clout, though, for he did manage to land that spittoon alongside Tuggle's jaw with some weight behind it. Tuggle let out a bleat and his eyes rolled up and out he went like a candle in a windstorm. Wasn't nothing I could do then but let Peckham have another whack with my bungstarter, this one on the back of his noggin, which put *him* out cold, too, athwart Tuggle.

The other patrons crowded up and we all looked down at them two sorry specimens. What a sight they was, lying there all bloody and bruised, fancy clothes in tatters, with not a lick of dignity left to either one. And all on account of some danged patent medicines that likely couldn't cure one in fifty of the ills and afflictions they was supposed to. Including and especially loss of manhood.

Harry Weems, the night clerk back then, was gawping in from the hotel lobby, and I hollered to him to run and fetch the sheriff. Then I went back around the bar for a swallow of something to settle my nerves. Not hardly Cherokee's Magical Herb Bitters and not hardly Dr. Wallmann's Celebrated Nerve and Brain Tonic. No sir—good old bourbon whiskey.

Now while we all waited for the sheriff, one of the regular customers picked up them two brown bottles that was setting side by side on the bartop and looked close at the labels. Then he let out a whoop and handed the bottles to me. And when I had a close look myself, what do you think I seen?

Why, both snake oils was manufactured by the John C. Delacroix Company of Chicago, Illinois. The same dang company! And neither of them peckerwoods had a clue until they woke up in jail together and the sheriff informed 'em.

Didn't I tell you old-time drummers was a caution?

No Room at the Inn

W HEN THE snowstorm started, Quincannon was high up in a sparsely populated section of the Sierra Nevada—alone except for his rented horse, with not much idea of where he was and no idea at all of where Slick Henry Garber was.

And as if all of that wasn't enough, it was almost nightfall on Christmas Eve.

The storm had caught him by surprise. The winter sky had been clear when he'd set out from Big Creek in mid-morning, and it had stayed clear until two hours ago; then the clouds had commenced piling up rapidly, the way they sometimes did in this high-mountain country, getting thicker and darker-veined until the whole sky was the color of moiling coal smoke. The wind had sharpened to an icy breath that buffeted both him and the ewe-necked strawberry roan. And now, at dusk, the snow flurries had begun—thick flakes driven and agitated by the wind so that the pine and spruce forests through which the trail climbed were a misty blur and he could see no more than forty or fifty feet ahead.

He rode huddled inside his fleece-lined long coat and rabbit-fur mittens and cap, feeling sorry for himself and at the same time cursing himself for a rattlepate. If he had paid more mind to that buildup of clouds, he would have realized the need to find shelter much sooner than he had. As it was, he had begun looking too late. So far no cabin or mine shaft or cave or suitable geographical configuration had presented itself—not one place in all this vast wooded emptiness where he and the roan could escape the snapping teeth of the storm.

A man had no sense wandering around an unfamiliar mountain wilderness on the night before Christmas, even if he *was* a manhunter by trade and a greedy gloryhound by inclination. He ought to be home in front of a blazing fire, roasting chestnuts in the company of a good woman. Sabina, for instance. Dear, sweet Sabina, waiting for him back in San Francisco. Not by his hearth or in his bed, curse the luck, but at least in the Market Street offices of Carpenter and Quincannon, Professional Detective Services.

Well, it was his own fault that he was alone up here, freezing to death in a snowstorm. In the first place he could have refused the job of tracking down Slick Henry Garber when it was offered to him by the West Coast Banking Association two weeks ago. In the second place he could have decided not to come to Big Creek to investigate a report that Slick Henry and his satchel full of counterfeit mining stock were in the vicinity. And in the third place he could have remained in Big Creek this morning when Slick Henry managed to elude his clutches and flee even higher into these blasted mountains.

But no, Rattlepate John Quincannon had done none of those sensible things. Instead he had accepted the Banking Association's fat fee, thinking only of that *and* of the additional $5000 reward for Slick Henry's apprehension or demise being offered by a mining coalition in Colorado *and* of the glory of nabbing the most notorious—and the most dangerous—confidence trickster operating west of the Rockies in this year of 1894. Then, after tracing his quarry to Big Creek, he had not only bungled the arrest but made a second mistake in setting out on Slick Henry's trail with the sublime confidence of an unrepentent sinner looking for the Promised Land—only to lose that trail two hours ago, at a road fork, just before he made his *third* mistake of the day by underestimating the weather.

Christmas, he thought. 'Tis the season to be jolly. Bah. Humbug.

Ice particles now clung to his beard, his eyebrows; kept trying to freeze his eyelids shut. He had to continually rub his eyes clear in order to see where he was going. Which, now, in full darkness, was along the rim of a snow-skinned meadow that had opened up on his left. The wind was even fiercer here, without one wall of trees to deflect some of its force. Quincannon shivered and huddled and cursed and felt sorrier for himself by the minute.

He should never have decided to join forces with Sabina and open a detective agency. She had been happy with her position as a female operative with the Pinkerton Agency's Denver office; he had been more or less content working in the San Francisco office of the United States Secret Service. What had possessed him to suggest, not long after their first professional meeting, that they pool their talents? Well, he knew the answer to that well enough. *Sabina* had possessed him. Dear, sweet, unseducible, infuriating Sabina—

Was that light ahead?

He scrubbed at his eyes and leaned forward in the saddle, squinting. Yes, light—lamplight. He had just come around a jog in the trail, away from the open meadow, and there it was, ahead on his right: a faint glowing rectangle in the night's churning white-and-black. He could just make out the shapes of buildings, too, in what appeared to be a clearing before a sheer rock face.

The lamplight and the buildings changed Quincannon's bleak remonstrations into murmurs of thanksgiving. He urged the stiff-legged and balky roan into a quicker pace. The buildings took on shape and definition as he approached. There were three of them, grouped in a loose triangle; two appeared to be cabins, fashioned of rough-hewn logs and planks, each with a sloping roof, while the bulkiest structure had the look of a barn. The larger cabin, the one with the lighted window, was set between the other two and farther back near the base of the rock wall.

A lane led off the trail to the buildings. Quincannon couldn't see it under its covering of snow, but he knew it was there by a painted board sign nailed to one of the trees at the intersection. *TRAVELER'S REST*, the sign said, and below that, in smaller letters, *Meals and Lodging*. One of the tiny roadhouses, then, that dotted the Sierras and catered to prospectors, hunters, and foolish wilderness wayfarers such as himself.

It was possible, he thought as he turned past the sign, that Slick Henry Garber had come this way and likewise been drawn to the Traveler's Rest. Which would allow Quincannon to make amends today, after all, for his earlier bungling, and perhaps even permit him to spend Christmas Day in the relative comfort of the Big Creek Hotel. Given his recent run of foul luck, however, such a serendipitous turnabout was as likely to happen as Sabina presenting him, on his return to San Francisco, with the holiday gift he most desired.

Nevertheless, caution here was indicated. So despite the warmth promised by the lamplit window, he rode at an off-angle toward the barn. There was also the roan's welfare to consider. He would have to pay for the animal if it froze to death while in his charge.

If he was being observed from within the lighted cabin, it was covertly: no one came out and no one showed himself in the window. At the barn he dismounted, took himself and the roan inside, struggled to reshut the doors against the howling thrust of the wind. Blackness surrounded him, heavy with the smells of animals and hay and oiled leather. He stripped off both mittens, found a lucifer in one of his pockets and scraped it alight. The barn lantern hung from a hook near the doors; he reached up to light the wick. Now he could see that there were

NO ROOM AT THE INN

eight stalls, half of which were occupied: three saddle horses and one work horse, each nibbling a pile of hay. He didn't bother to examine the saddle horses because he had no idea what type of animal Slick Henry had been riding. He hadn't got close enough to his quarry all day to get a look at him or his transportation.

He led the roan into an empty stall, unsaddled it, left it there munching a hay supper of its own. Later, he would ask the owner of Traveler's Rest to come out and give the beast a proper rubdown. With his hands mittened again he braved the storm on foot, slogging through calf-deep snow to the lighted cabin.

Still no one came out or appeared at the window. He moved along the front wall, stopped to peer through the rimed window glass. What he could see of the big parlor inside was uninhabited. He plowed ahead to the door.

It was against his nature to walk unannounced into the home of a stranger, mainly because it was a fine way to get shot, but in this case he had no choice. He could have shouted himself hoarse in competition with the storm before anyone heard him. Thumping on the door would be just as futile; the wind was already doing that. Again he stripped off his right mitten, opened his coat for easy access to the Remington Navy revolver he carried at his waist, unlatched the door with his left hand, and cautiously let the wind push him inside.

The entire parlor was deserted. He leaned back hard against the door to get it closed again and then called out, "Hello the house! Company!" No one answered.

He stood scraping snowcake off his face, slapping it off his clothing. The room was warm: a log fire crackled merrily on the hearth, banking somewhat because it hadn't been fed in a while. Two lamps were lit in here, another in what looked to be a dining room adjacent. Near the hearth, a cut spruce reached almost to the raftered ceiling; it was festooned with Christmas decorations—strung popcorn and bright-colored beads, stubs of tallow candles in bent can tops, snippets of fleece from some old garment sprinkled on the branches to resemble snow, a five-pointed star atop the uppermost branch.

All very cozy and inviting, but where were the occupants? He called out again, and again received no response. He cocked his head to listen. Heard only the plaint of the storm and the snicking of flung snow against the windowpane—no sound at all within the cabin.

He crossed the parlor, entered the dining room. The puncheon table was set for two, and in fact two people had been eating there not so long ago. A clay pot of venison stew sat in the center of the table; when he touched it he found it and its contents still slightly warm. Ladlings of stew and slices of bread were on each of the two plates.

The hair began to pull along the nape of his neck, as it always did when he sensed a wrongness to things. Slick Henry? Or something else? With his hand now gripping the butt of his Navy, he eased his way through a doorway at the rear of the dining room.

Kitchen and larder. Stove still warm, a kettle atop it blackening smokily because all the water it had contained had boiled away. Quincannon transferred the kettle to the sink drainboard. Moved then to another closed door that must lead to a bedroom, the last of the cabin's rooms. He depressed the latch and pushed the door wide.

Bedroom, indeed. And as empty as the other three rooms. But there were two odd things here: The sash of a window in the far wall was raised a few inches; and on the floor was the base of a lamp that had been dropped or knocked off the bedside table. Snow coated the window sill and there was a sifting of it on the floor and on the lamp base.

Quincannon stood puzzled and scowling in the icy draft. No room at the inn? he thought ironically. On the contrary, there was plenty of room at this inn on Christmas Eve. It didn't seem to have *any* people in it.

On a table near the bed he spied a well-worn family Bible. Impulse took him to it; he opened it at the front, where such vital statistics as marriages, births, and deaths were customarily recorded. Two names were written there in a fine woman's hand: Martha and Adam Keene. And a wedding date: July 17, 1893. That was all.

Well, now he knew the identity of the missing occupants. But what had happened to them? He hadn't seen them in the barn. And the other, smaller cabin—guest accommodations, he judged—had also been in darkness upon his arrival. It made no sense that a man and his wife would suddenly quit the warmth of their home in the middle of a Christmas Eve supper, to lurk about in a darkened outbuilding. It also made no sense that they would voluntarily decide to rush off into a snowstorm on foot or on horseback. Forced out of here, then? By Slick Henry Garber or someone else? If so, *why*?

Quincannon returned to the parlor. He had no desire to go out again into the wind and swirling snow, but he was not the sort of man who could allow a confounding mystery to go uninvestigated—particularly a mystery that might involve a criminal with a handsome price on his head. So, grumbling a little, his unmittened hands deep in the pockets of his coat, he bent his body into what was swiftly becoming a full-scale blizzard.

He fought his way to the barn first, because it was closer and to satisfy himself that it really *was* occupied only by horses. The wind had blown out the lantern when he'd left earlier; he relighted it, but not until he had first drawn his revolver. One of the animals—not the rented roan—moved restlessly in its stall as he walked toward the far end. There were good-sized piles of hay in each of the empty stalls as well, he noticed. He leaned into those stalls with the lantern. If anyone were hiding in a haypile it would have to be close to the surface to avoid the risk of suffocation; he poked at each pile in turn with the Navy's barrel. Hay and nothing but hay.

In one corner of the back wall was an enclosure that he took to be a harness room. Carefully he opened the door with his gun hand. Buckles and bit chains gleamed in the narrow space within; he saw the shapes of saddles, bridles, hackamores. Something made a scurrying noise among the floor shadows and he lowered the lantern in time to see the tail end of a packrat disappear behind a loose board. Dust was the only other thing on the floor.

He went back toward the front, stopped again when he was abreast of the loft ladder. He climbed it with the lantern lifted above his head. But the loft contained nothing more than several tightly stacked bales of hay and a thin scattering of straw that wouldn't have concealed the packrat, much less a man or a woman.

No one in the main cabin, no one in the barn. That left only the guest cabin. And if that, too, was deserted? Well, then, he thought irascibly, he would sit down in the main cabin and gorge himself on venison stew while he waited for somebody— the Keenes, Slick Henry, the Ghost of Christmas Past—to put in an appearance. He was cold and tired and hungry, and mystery or no mystery he was not about to wander around in a blizzard hunting for clues.

Out once more into the white fury. By the time he worked his way through what were now thigh-deep drifts to the door of the guest cabin, his legs and arms were stiff and his beard was caked with frozen snow. He wasted no time getting the door open, but he didn't enter right away. Instead he let the wind hurl the door inward, so that it cracked audibly against the wall, while he hung back and to one side with his revolver drawn.

Nothing happened inside.

He waited another few seconds, but already the icebound night was beginning to numb his bare hand; another minute or two of exposure and the skin would freeze to the gunmetal. He entered the cabin in a sideways crouch, caught hold of the door and crowded it shut until it latched. Chill, clotted black encased him now, so thick that he was virtually blind. Should he risk lighting a match? Well, if he wanted to see who or what this cabin might contain, he would *have* to risk it. Floundering around in the dark would no doubt mean a broken limb, his luck being what it was these days.

He fumbled in his pocket for another lucifer, struck it on his left thumbnail, ducked down and away from the flare of light. Still nothing happened. But the light revealed that this cabin was divided into two sparsely furnished bedrooms with an open door in the dividing wall; and it also revealed some sort of huddled mass on the floor of the rear bedroom.

In slow strides, holding the match up and away from his body, he moved toward the doorway. The flame died just as he reached it—just as he recognized the huddled mass as the motionless body of a man. He thumbed another match alight, went through the doorway, leaned down for a closer look. The man lay drawn up on his back, and on one temple blood from a bullet furrow glistened blackly in the wavering flame. Young man, sandy-haired, wearing an old vicuna cloth suit and a clean white shirt now spotted with blood. A man Quincannon had never seen before—

Something moved behind him.

Something else slashed the air, grazed the side of Quincannon's head as he started to turn and dodge, drove him sideways to the floor.

The lucifer went out as he was struck; he lost his grip on the Navy and it went clattering away into blackness as thick as the inside of Old Scratch's fundament. The blow had been sharp enough to set up a ringing in his ears, but the thick rabbit-fur cap had cushioned it enough so that he wasn't stunned. He pulled around onto his knees, lunged back toward the doorway with both hands reaching. Above him he heard again that slashing of the air, only this time the swung object missed him entirely. Which threw the man who had swung off balance, at the same instant Quincannon's right hand found a grip on sheepskin material not unlike that of his own coat. He yanked hard, heard a grunt, and then the heavy weight of his assailant came squirming and cursing down on top of him.

The floor of an unfamiliar, black-dark room was the last place Quincannon would have chosen for hand-to-hand combat. But he was a veteran of any number of skirmishes, and had learned ways to do grievous damage to an opponent that would have shocked the Marquis of Queensbury. (Sabina, too, no doubt). Besides which, this particular opponent, whoever he was, was laboring under the same disadvantages as he was.

There were a few seconds of scrambling and bumping about, some close-quarters pummeling on both sides, a blow that split Quincannon's lip and made his Scot's blood boil even more furiously, a brief and violent struggle for possession of what felt like a long-barreled revolver, and then, finally, an opportunity for Quincannon to use a mean and scurrilous trick he had learned in a free-for-all on the Baltimore docks. His assailant screamed, quit fighting, began to twitch instead; and to groan and wail and curse feebly. This vocal combination made Quincannon's head hurt all the more, and led him, since he now had possession of the long-barreled revolver, to thump the man on top of the head with the weapon. The groaning and wailing and cursing ceased apruptly. So did the twitching.

Quincannon got to his feet, stood shakily wiping blood from his torn lip. He made the mistake then of taking a blind step and almost fell over one or the other of the two men now lying motionless on the floor. He produced another lucifer from his dwindling supply. In its flare he spied a lamp, and managed to get to it in time to light the wick before the flame died. He located his Navy, holstered it, then carried the lamp to where the men lay and peered at the face of the one who had tried to brain him.

"Well, well," he said aloud, with considerable relish. "A serendipitous turnabout after all. Just what I wanted for Christmas—Slick Henry Garber."

Slick Henry Garber said nothing, nor would he be able to for a good while.

The young, sandy-haired lad—Adam Keene, no doubt—was also unconscious. The bullet wound on his head didn't seem to be serious, but he would need attention. *He* wouldn't be saying anything, either, for a good while. Quincannon would just have to wait for the full story of what had happened here before his arrival. Unless, of course, he got it from Adam Keene's wife . . .

Where *was* Adam Keene's wife?

Carrying the lamp, he searched the two bedrooms. No sign of Martha Keene. He did find Slick Henry's leather satchel, in a corner of the rear room; it contained several thousand shares of bogus mining stock and nine thousand dollars in greenbacks. He also found evidence of a struggle, and not one but two bullet holes in the back wall.

These things, plus a few others, plus a belated application of imagination and logic, allowed him to make a reasonably accurate guess as to tonight's sequence of events. Slick Henry had arrived just before the snowstorm and just as the Keenes were sitting down to supper. He had either put his horse in the barn himself or Adam Keene had done it; that explained why there had been *three* saddle horses present when only *two* people lived at Traveler's Rest. Most likely Slick Henry had then thrown down on the Keenes: he must have been aware that Quincannon was still close behind him, even if Quincannon hadn't known it, and must have realized that with the

NO ROOM AT THE INN

impending storm it was a good bet his pursuer would also stop at Traveler's Rest. And what better place for an ambush than one of these three buildings? Perhaps he'd chosen the guest cabin on the theory that Quincannon would be less on his guard there than at the other two. To ensure that, Slick Henry had taken Adam Keene with him at gunpoint, leaving Mrs. Keene in the main cabin with instructions to tell Quincannon that no other travelers had appeared today and to then send him to the guest cabin.

But while the two men were in that cabin Adam Keene had heroically attempted to disarm Slick Henry, there had been a struggle, and Keene had unheroically received a bullet wound for his efforts. Martha Keene must have heard at least one of the shots, and fearing the worst she had left the main cabin through the bedroom window and hidden herself somewhere. Had Slick Henry found her? Not likely. But it seemed reasonable to suppose he had been out hunting for her when Quincannon came. The violence of the storm had kept him from springing his trap at that point; he had decided instead to return to the guest cabin as per his original plan. And this was where he had been ever since, waiting in the dark for his nemesis to walk in like a damned fool—which was just what Quincannon had done.

This day's business, Quincannon thought ruefully, had been one long, grim comedy of errors on all sides. Slick Henry's actions were at least half doltish and so were his own. Especially his own—blundering in half a dozen different ways, including not even once considering the possibility of a planned ambush. Relentless manhunter, intrepid detective. Bah. It was a wonder he hadn't been shot dead. Sabina would chide him mercilessly if he told her the entire story of his capture of Slick Henry Garber. Which, of course, he had no intention of doing.

Well, he could redeem himself somewhat by finding Martha

Keene. Almost certainly she had to be in one of the three buildings. She wouldn't have remained in the open, exposed, in a raging mountain storm. She would not have come anywhere near the guest cabin because of Slick Henry. And she hadn't stayed in the main cabin; the open bedroom window proved that. Ergo, she was in the barn. But he had searched the barn, even gone up into the hayloft. No place to hide up there, or in the harness enclosure, or in one of the stalls, or—

The lamp base on the bedroom floor, he thought.

No room at the inn, he thought.

"Well, of course, you blasted rattlepate," he said aloud. "It's the only place she *can* be."

Out once more into the whipping snow and freezing wind (after first taking the precaution of binding Slick Henry's hands with the man's own belt). Slog, slog, slog, and finally into the darkened barn. He lighted the lantern, took it to the approximate middle of the building, and then called out, "Mrs. Keene! My name is John Quincannon, I am a detective from San Francisco, and I have just cracked the skull of the man who terrorized you and your husband tonight. You have nothing more to fear."

No response.

"I know you're here, and approximately where. Won't you save both of us the embarrassment of my poking around with a pitchfork?"

Silence.

"Mrs. Keene, your husband is unconscious with a head wound and he needs you. Please believe me."

More silence. Then, just as he was about to issue another plea, there was a rustling and stirring in one of the empty stalls to his left. He moved over that way in time to see Martha Keene rise up slowly from her hiding place deep under the pile of hay.

She was young, attractive, as fair-haired as her husband, and wrapped warmly in a heavy fleece-lined coat. She was also, Quincannon noted with surprise, quite obviously with child.

What didn't surprise him was the length of round, hollow glass she held in one hand—the chimney that belonged to the lamp base on the bedroom floor. She had had the presence of mind to snatch it up before climbing out of the window, in her haste dislodging the base from the bedside table. The chimney was the reason neither he nor Slick Henry had found her; by using it as a breathing tube, she had been able to burrow deep enough into the haypile to escape a superficial search.

For a space she stared at Quincannon out of wide, anxious eyes. What she saw seemed to reassure her. She released a thin, sighing breath and said tremulously, "My husband . . . you're sure he's not—?"

"No, no. Wounded I said and wounded I meant. He'll soon be good as new."

"Thank God!"

"And you, my dear? Are you all right?"

"Yes, I . . . yes. Just frightened. I've been lying here imagining all sorts of dreadful things." Mrs. Keene sighed again, plucked clinging straw from her face and hair. "I didn't *want* to run and hide, but I thought Adam must be dead and I was afraid for my baby . . . oh!" She winced as if with a sudden sharp pain, dropped the lamp chimney and placed both hands over the swell of her abdomen. "All the excitement . . . I believe the baby will arrive sooner than expected."

Quincannon gave her a horrified look. "Right here? *Now*?"

"No, not that soon." A wan smile. "Tomorrow . . ."

It was his turn to put forth a relieved sigh as he moved into the stall to help her up. Tomorrow. Christmas Day. Appropriate that she should have her baby then. But it wasn't the only thing about this situation that was appropriate to the season. This was a stable, and what was the stall where she had lain with her unborn child but a manger? There were animals in attendance, too. And at least one wise man (wise in *some* things, surely) who had come bearing a gift without even knowing it, a gift of a third—no, a half—of the $5000 reward for the capture of Slick Henry Garber.

Peace on earth, good will to men.

Quincannon smiled; of a sudden he felt very jolly and very much in a holiday spirit. This was, he thought, going to be a fine Christmas after all.

The Western Pulps

For much of the first half of this century, pulp magazines were the leading supplier of popular fiction to the masses—not only in the United States but in Canada and England as well. They were seven by ten inches in size, printed on untrimmed woodpulp paper, and had gaudy enameled covers that depicted scenes of high melodrama. The stories they contained were (for the most part) just as gaudy and melodramatic as their artwork. Successors to the dime novels and story weeklies of the nineteenth century, they were mass-produced to provide inexpensive escapist reading for imaginative young adults and the so-called "common man," selling for a nickel or a dime in their early years and a quarter in their final ones. At the height of their popularity, in the mid-thirties, there were more than 200 different titles on the market—magazines specializing in stories of mystery, detection, adventure, war on land and sea and in the air, life (and death) in the Old West, sports, romance, science fiction, fantasy, and sometimes sadistic horror.

Far and away the most popular pulps were Westerns. Such titles as *Western Story*, *Wild West Weekly*, *Ranch Romances*, *Texas Rangers*, and *Dime Western* perennially outsold those in all other categories throughout most of the pulp era. This is hardly surprising when one considers that the Western story is a uniquely American art form, and that as a result Americans have not only embraced fictional chronicles of the great westward expansion, but elevated them to the lofty status of myth.

During this century the Western has been a symbol of all that America stands for: freedom, justice, self-reliance, the pioneer spirit. And in the Depression thirties and the war-torn forties, Americans *needed* that myth, that spirit to sustain them. The Western pulps, then, were more than just cheap entertainment, more than just an escape into the past; they were a hope for the future.

The first Western pulp was established by Street & Smith, the dime-novel kings. In 1919 S&S revamped one of their dime-novel periodicals, *New Buffalo Bill Weekly*, into the pulp format and retitled the new bi-weekly *Western Story Magazine*. (At that time pulp magazines had been around for nearly twenty years. Frank A. Munsey had restructured *Argosy* into a pulp in the mid-1890s, and soon afterward brought out numerous other pulp titles, among them *All-Story Weekly*, *Popular Magazine*, and *The Railroad Man's Magazine*.) The circulation of *Western Story*, which sold for ten cents, burgeoned in the twenties, when Street & Smith made it into a weekly, and it remained one of the two or three top-selling titles throughout its three decades of life.

One of the primary reasons for *Western Story*'s success was the authentic Western flavor of the stories it published— stories by such born-and-bred Westerners as Walt Coburn, W. C. Tuttle, Stephen Payne, Jay Lucas, Ney N. Geer, and Raymond S. Spears. And yet, ironically, the most popular *Western Story* author by far was an Eastern intellectual and frustrated poet, Frederick Faust, better known as Max Brand. Writing as Brand, George Owen Baxter, Evan Evans, and David Manning, among other names, Faust was the undisputed king of the Western pulps, publishing over 300 book-length Western serials and hundreds of shorter works in a career that spanned slightly more than two decades. (He also published hundreds of adventure, mystery, historical romance, medical, and science fiction pulp novels and stories.) In the twenties and thirties he wrote as much as two-thirds of some issues of *Western Story*, often having two or three serials running concurrently. The reason for his popularity, aside from an innate ability to create fascinating characters and storylines full of nonstop action, was what one critic has described as a "leap of Faustian imagination . . . that urges the story beyond the established borders of the Western and into a vaguer territory of fantasy and universal myth."

The success of *Western Story* inspired imitations and variations, of course. Doubleday brought out *West* and *Frontier Stories*, which would also prove to be long-running titles; William Clayton started *Cowboy Stories*, *Ace-High Western*, *Ranch Romances*, and *Western Adventures*; Fiction House produced *Lariat*; and Street & Smith added *Far West*, *Wild West Weekly*, and *Pete Rice Magazine* to its stable. (Pistol Pete Rice, a rough-and-tumble Arizona sheriff with a coterie of deputies, was the first Western pulp hero to have his own magazine.) In the 1930s Ned Pines and his editorial director, Leo Margulies, started the Thrilling Group, which included such titles as *Thrilling Western*, *Popular Western*, *Texas Rangers*, and three Pete Rice rivals: *Masked Rider*, *Range Riders*, and *Rio Kid*. Harry Steeger's Popular Publications, eventually the largest and most active of the pulp chain publishers, also jumped on the bandwagon with *Dime Western*, *.44 Western*, *New Western*, *Star Western*, and *Big-Book Western*, among others. And there were numerous other titles produced by independent and small-chain outfits, some of which flourished for a while but most of which were short-lived; among these were *Ace Western* and *Mammoth Western*.

A successful adjunct to the Western pulps of this period were those magazines devoted wholly or in large part to "Northerns"—stories set in the wide-open frontier days of Alaska, the Yukon, and the Canadian Barrens. The first and most popular of these was Fiction House's *North-West Stories* (later *Northwest Romances*), which in its early years proclaimed itself "the world's only all Western and Northern story magazine," and modestly announced that what it published were "vigorous, tingling epics of the great *Snow* FRONTIER and the IMMORTAL WEST!" The magazine lasted more than twenty-five years and featured the work of such writers as Jack London, Robert W. Service, James B. Hendryx, William Byron Mowery, W. Ryerson Johnson, and Dan Cushman. Northerns also appeared frequently in such Western pulps as *Western Story*; and of course both Westerns and Northerns were regularly featured in *Argosy*, *Adventure*, *Short Stories*, and other adventure pulps.

The paper shortage of World War II killed off a large number of pulp titles, including many marginal Western books. Of the survivors, a handful were purchased by the healthier chain publishers such as Popular and Thrilling and thus underwent changes in editorial policy. A few new titles were introduced during and after the war, and into the early fifties, among them two named after Western pulp giants: *Max Brand's Western Magazine* and *Walt Coburn's Western Magazine*. But the handwriting was on the wall: the pulps were doomed. The advent of war may have ended the Depression in this country, but it also began the decline and fall of the pulp kingdom; and in the war's aftermath, things began to change rapidly and radically everywhere. The publishing industry was especially vulnerable. Television and paperback books were the coming forms of inexpensive entertainment for the masses; there was little room for the pulps in the new and changing society.

Most titles were extinct by 1950. A few hardy ones, most of them Westerns, hung on a few years longer: *Dime Western*, *Thrilling Western*, *Big-Book Western*, *Fifteen Western Tales*, and *.44 Western* until 1954; *Western Short Stories*, *Complete Western Book*, *Texas Rangers*, and *2-Gun Western* until 1957–58. *Ranch Romances*, amazingly enough, lasted until 1970 (though it was a mere shadow of itself at the end, publishing reprints almost exclusively), thus earning the distinction of being the longest surviving pulp title.

THE "DIGEST PULPS"

Although technically not pulp magazines, the digest-size Western periodicals of the past fifty years were in fact pulps in every major respect: aim, content, even the paper on which they were printed. The only appreciable difference was size.

The first digest Western was the short-lived *Pocket Western*, which appeared in the late thirties. (The title was revived in 1950 by Trojan Magazines, and again proved to be short-lived. So did a companion magazine, *Six-Gun Western*.) It was Street & Smith that had the first success with the digest format, during World War II when the paper shortage led to a decision to shrink such pulp titles as *Western Story* and *Romantic Range* (and *Detective Story*, *Doc Savage*, and *The Shadow*). The format proved so popular with readers that even after the war S&S continued to publish *Western Story* as a digest, until its demise in 1949.

Other publishers followed Street & Smith's lead in reducing full-sized pulps to the smaller size, though without nearly as much success. Early in 1950 Dell relaunched one of its old pulp titles, *All-Western*, as a digest, but it lasted only a few issues and ceased publication for good in 1951. Stadium Publishing briefly reduced *Best Western* in 1951, then returned it to the standard pulp format for the remaining few years of his life. And in 1958, Robert A.W. Lowndes' Columbia Publications shrank all of its pulp titles, among them *Famous Western*, *Double-Action Western*, *Western Action*, and *Real Western*. These remained digest-sized until their group demise in 1960.

The best of the Western magazines that began and ended

their lives in the digest format—and one of the best of all the Western fiction periodicals—commenced publication in November of 1946. This was *Zane Grey's Western Magazine*. Under the editorship of Don Ward, *ZGWM* published original fiction by most of the major names in the Western field, as well as classic reprints by Zane Grey, and a number of nonfiction features. Ward was especially good at developing new writers; among his "finds" were Elmore Leonard and Lewis B. Patten. (He also persuaded science fiction and fantasy writer Theodore Sturgeon to concoct a few Western stories, and later collaborated with Sturgeon on a couple of others.) Throughout its relatively short life—its final issue appeared early in 1954—*ZGWM* remained a showcase for some of the most interesting and entertaining short fiction of its era.

Another quality publication appeared in 1953 from Flying Eagle Publications: *Gunsmoke*, an "adult" Western magazine in that it offered stories of a much grimmer and more elemental nature than most pulp Western fare. (Flying Eagle was also the publisher of *Manhunt*, a successful crime-fiction magazine devoted to modern stories of the "seamier side of life.") Although *Gunsmoke* featured some outstanding stories, by such writers as Jack Schaefer, A.B. Guthrie, Jr., Frank O'Rourke, Elmore Leonard, Nelson Nye, H.A. DeRosso, Bill Gulick, and Evan Hunter, it lasted only two issues. Readers of the time were evidently not ready to embrace the seamier side of frontier life.

A few other digest Westerns appeared in the 1950s, among them *Luke Short's Western Magazine* (which was also edited by Don Ward), *TOPS in Western Stories*, *Blazing Guns Western Story Magazine*, *Western Magazine*, and *3-Book Western*. None of these survived more than three years, with the last and longest-lived of them—Harry Widmer's *Western Magazine*—ceasing publication late in 1957. In 1960 a pulp-size magazine called *Wagon Train*, after the then-popular TV show, made a one-issue appearance; it was the only Western fiction periodical to be published between mid-1960 and 1969, when Leo Margulies revived *Zane Grey Western Magazine* in a monthly digest-size format. The new *ZGWM* featured a novella in each issue based on such Zane Grey characters as Arizona Ames and Laramie Nelson and purportedly written by Grey's son, Romer; each issue also contained classic reprints, as well as new fiction. This version of *ZGWM* had a life of just under four years, only the first two of which were as a digest; in its final years it was transformed into the large, flat format of such magazines as *True West*, and devoted as much space to fact articles as to fiction.

In 1978, the California-based *Far West Magazine* commenced publication; but after a promising beginning (its first issue contained a new story by Louis L'Amour), poor distribution and a misguided change to the large, flat format doomed it to extinction. By 1981 the last Western fiction magazine was dead.

The pulps may be gone, but they are not forgotten. Not only did they provide entertainment for millions of readers; they provided a training ground for scores of writers who eventually went on to bigger and better literary endeavors. Stephen Crane, Jack London, Theodore Dreiser, Sinclair Lewis, Tennessee Williams, Horace McCoy, Paul Gallico, Dashiell Hammett, Raymond Chandler, Isaac Asimov, Ray Bradbury, Edgar Rice Burroughs, John D. MacDonald, Cornell Woolrich, John Jakes, Evan Hunter, Erle Stanley Gardner, and Rex Stout, among many others, wrote for the pulp-paper magazines. And in the Western field, in addition to those already mentioned, so did such luminaries as Louis L'Amour, Luke Short, William MacLeod Raine, Clarence E. Mulford, Ernest Haycox, Charles Alden Seltzer, Fred Gipson, Wayne D. Overholser, Frank Bonham, Norman A. Fox, Les Savage, Jr., Steve

Frazee, Tom W. Blackburn, William R. Cox, Elmer Kelton, John Reese, Todhunter Ballard, T.V. Olsen, and Clifton Adams.

Much pulp fiction was of poor quality, to be sure; the stories were hastily written—many by hacks and many more by amateurs in order to satisfy the annual demand for millions upon millions of words during the boom years. But there is also much that is of quality, surprisingly high quality in some instances; much that has been reprinted in anthologies and single-author collections unto the present, for the entertainment of modern readers and the enlightenment of popular-culture scholars.

It is no exaggeration to say that if the Western pulps had never existed, popular Western literature would not be nearly as rich or as vital as it is today.

Bibliography of Books By Bill Pronzini

WESTERN PUBLICATIONS

Novels:

The Gallows Land. New York: Walker, 1983.
Starvation Camp. New York: Doubleday, 1984.
Quincannon. New York: Walker, 1985.
The Last Days of Horse-Shy Halloran. New York: M. Evans, 1987.
The Hangings. New York: Walker, 1989.
Firewind. New York: M. Evans, 1989.

Novels with Jeffrey Wallmann, as by William Jeffrey:

Duel at Gold Buttes. New York: Tower, 1981.
Border Fever. New York: Leisure, 1983.

Anthologies:

Wild Westerns. New York: Walker, 1986.
More Wild Westerns. New York: Walker, 1989.

Anthologies Co-edited with Martin H. Greenberg:

The Arbor House Treasury of Great Western Stories. New York: Arbor House, 1982.

The Western Hall of Fame. New York: Morrow, 1984.
The Lawmen. New York: Fawcett, 1984.
The Outlaws. New York: Fawcett, 1984.
The Reel West. New York: Doubleday, 1984.
The Cowboys. New York: Fawcett, 1985.
The Warriors. New York: Fawcett, 1985.
The Second Reel West. New York: Doubleday, 1985.
The Railroaders. New York: Fawcett, 1986.
The Third Reel West. New York: Doubleday, 1986.
The Steamboaters. New York: Fawcett, 1986.
The Cattlemen. New York: Fawcett, 1987.
The Horse Soldiers. New York: Fawcett, 1987.
The Gunfighters. New York: Fawcett, 1988.
The Texans. New York: Fawcett, 1988.
The Californians. New York: Fawcett, 1989.
The Arizonans. New York: Fawcett, 1989.
New Frontiers I. New York: Tor, 1990.
The Northerners. New York: Fawcett, 1990.

Anthology Co-Edited with Marcia Muller:

She Won the West. New York: Morrow, 1985.

Single-Author Collections Co-edited with Martin H. Greenberg:

The Best Western Stories of Steve Frazee. Carbondale, IL: Southern Illinois University Press, 1984; Ohio University Press, 1989.
The Best Western Stories of Wayne D. Overholser. Carbondale, IL: Southern Illinois University Press, 1984; Ohio University Press, 1989.
The Best Western Stories of Lewis B. Patten. Carbondale, IL: Southern Illinois University Press, 1987.

The Best Western Stories of Loren D. Estleman. Athens, Ohio: Ohio University Press, 1989.
The Best Western Stories of Frank Bonham. Athens, Ohio: Ohio University Press, 1989.

OTHER PUBLICATIONS

Novels:

The Stalker. New York: Random House, 1971.
Panic! New York: Random House, 1972.
A Run in Diamonds, as by Alex Saxon. New York: Pocket Books, 1973.
Snowbound. New York: Putnam's, 1974.
Games. New York: Putnam's, 1976.
The Cambodia File, with Jack Anderson. New York: Doubleday, 1981.
Masques. New York: Arbor House, 1981.
Day of the Moon, with Jeffrey Wallmann as by William Jeffrey. London: Robert Hale, 1983.
The Eye, with John Lutz. New York: Mysterious Press, 1984.
Beyond the Grave, with Marcia Muller. New York: Walker, 1986.
The Lighthouse, with Marcia Muller. New York: St. Martin's, 1987.

"Nameless Detective" Novels:

The Snatch. New York: Random House, 1972.
The Vanished. New York: Random House, 1973.
Undercurrent. New York: Random House, 1973.
Blowback. New York: Random House, 1977.
Twospot, with Collin Wilcox. New York: Putnam's, 1978.

Labyrinth. New York: St. Martin's, 1980.
Hoodwink. New York: New York: St. Martin's, 1981.
Scattershot. New York: St. Martin's, 1982.
Dragonfire. New York: St. Martin's, 1982.
Bindlestiff. New York: St. Martin's, 1983.
Quicksilver. New York: St. Martin's, 1984.
Double, with Marcia Muller. New York: St. Martin's, 1984.
Nightshades. New York: St. Martin's, 1984.
Bones. New York: St. Martin's, 1985.
Deadfall. New York: St. Martin's, 1986.
Shackles. New York: St. Martin's, 1988.
Jackpot. New York: Delacorte, 1990.

Novels as by Jack Foxx:

The Jade Figurine. New York: Bobbs-Merrill, 1972.
Dead Run. New York: Bobbs-Merrill, 1975.
Freebooty. New York: Bobbs-Merrill, 1976.
Wildfire. New York: Bobbs-Merrill, 1978.

Novels with Barry N. Malzberg:

The Running of Beasts. New York: Putnam's, 1976.
Acts of Mercy. New York: Putnam's, 1977.
Night Screams. New York: Playboy Press, 1979.
Prose Bowl. New York: St. Martin's, 1980.

Short-Story Collections:

Casefile: The Best of the "Nameless Detective" Stories. New York: St. Martin's, 1983.
Graveyard Plots. New York: St. Martin's, 1985.
Small Felonies. New York: St. Martin's, 1988.

Nonfiction Books:

Gun in Cheek. New York: Coward McCann, 1982.
1001 Midnights: The Aficionado's Guide to Mystery and Detective Fiction, with Marcia Muller. New York: Arbor House, 1986.
Son of Gun in Cheek. New York: Mysterious Press, 1987.

Anthologies:

Tricks and Treats, co-edited with Joe Gores. New York: Doubleday, 1976.
Midnight Specials. New York: Bobbs-Merrill, 1977.
Werewolf! New York: Arbor House, 1979.
The Edgar Winners. New York: Random House, 1980.
Voodoo! New York: Arbor House, 1980.
Mummy! New York: Arbor House, 1980.
Creature! New York: Arbor House, 1981.
The Arbor House Necropolis. New York: Arbor House, 1981.
Specter! New York: Arbor House, 1982.
The Arbor House Treasury of Detective and Mystery Stories from the Great Pulps. New York: Arbor House, 1983.

Anthologies Co-edited with Martin H. Greenberg:

The Mystery Hall of Fame. New York: Morrow, 1984.
13 Short Mystery Novels. New York: Greenwich House, 1985.
A Treasury of Civil War Stories. New York: Bonanza, 1985.
A Treasury of World War II Stories. New York: Bonanza, 1985.
Murder in the First Reel. New York: Avon, 1985.
The Ethnic Detectives. New York: Dodd, Mead, 1985.
Women Sleuths. Chicago: Academy Chicago, 1985.
Police Procedurals. Chicago: Academy Chicago, 1985.

Great Modern Police Stories. New York: Walker, 1986.
101 Mystery Stories. New York: Avenel, 1986.
Locked Room Puzzles. Chicago: Academy Chicago, 1986.
Prime Suspects. New York: Ivy Books, 1987.
Uncollected Crimes. New York: Walker, 1987.
Suspicious Characters. New York: Ivy Books, 1987.
Manhattan Mysteries. New York: Avenel, 1987.
Criminal Elements. New York: Ivy Books, 1988.
13 Short Detective Novels. New York: Bonanza, 1988.
Cloak and Dagger. New York: Avenel, 1988.
The Mammoth Book of Private Eye Stories. New York: Carroll & Graf, 1988.
Homicidal Acts. New York: Ivy Books, 1989.
Felonious Assaults. New York: Ivy Books, 1989.

Anthology Co-edited with Martin H. Greenberg and Marcia Muller:

Lady on the Case. New York: Bonanza, 1988.

Anthologies Co-edited with Martin H. Greenberg and Barry N. Malzberg:

The Arbor House Treasury of Horror & the Supernatural. New York: Arbor House, 1981.
The Arbor House Treasury of Mystery & Suspense. New York: Arbor House, 1981.
Mystery in the Mainstream. New York: Morrow, 1986.

Anthologies Co-edited with Barry N. Malzberg:

Dark Sins, Dark Dreams. New York: Doubleday, 1978.
The End of Summer. New York: Ace Books, 1979.
Shared Tomorrows. New York: St. Martin's, 1979.
Bug-Eyed Monsters. New York: Harcourt Brace, 1980.

Anthologies Co-edited with Marcia Muller:

The Web She Weaves. New York: Morrow, 1983.
Child's Ploy. New York: Macmillan, 1984.
Witches' Brew. New York: Macmillan, 1984.
Chapter and Hearse. New York: Morrow, 1985.
Dark Lessons. New York: Macmillan, 1985.
Kill or Cure. New York: Macmillan, 1985.
The Wickedest Show on Earth. New York: Morrow, 1985.
The Deadly Arts. New York: Arbor House, 1985.

A Note about the Author

A full-time professional fiction writer since 1969, Bill Pronzini has published eight novels and numerous short stories and fact pieces in the Western genre; he has also edited or co-edited more than a score of Western fiction anthologies and single-author collections, including five previous volumes in Swallow Press's "Best Western Stories of . . ." series. Among his other works are 34 mystery and suspense novels, one mainstream novel (written in collaboration with political columnist Jack Anderson), three volumes of short stories, and three non-fiction works. He is the recipient of numerous awards, among them the Life Achievement Award (presented in 1987) from the Private Eye Writers of America.